camp CONFIDENTIAL

A Fair to Remember

GROSSET & DUNLAP
Published by the Penguin Group
Penguin Group (USA) Inc., 375 Hudson Street, New York,
New York 10014, U.S.A.
Penguin Group (Canada), 90 Eglinton Avenue East, Suite 700, Toronto,
Ontario, Canada M4P 2Y3 (a division of Pearson Penguin Canada Inc.)
Penguin Books Ltd, 80 Strand, London WC2R 0RL, England
Penguin Ireland, 25 St Stephen's Green, Dublin 2, Ireland
(a division of Penguin Books Ltd)
Penguin Group (Australia), 250 Camberwell Road, Camberwell, Victoria 3124,
Australia (a division of Pearson Australia Group Pty Ltd)
Penguin Books India Pvt Ltd, 11 Community Centre, Panchsheel Park,
New Delhi - 110 017, India
Penguin Group (NZ), Cnr Airborne and Rosedale Roads, Albany,
Auckland 1310, New Zealand (a division of Pearson New Zealand Ltd)
Penguin Books (South Africa) (Pty) Ltd, 24 Sturdee Avenue, Rosebank,
Johannesburg 2196, South Africa

Penguin Books Ltd, Registered Offices:
80 Strand, London WC2R 0RL, England

Cover designed by Ching N. Chan.

Front cover image © Image Source/Image Source/Getty Images.
Text copyright © 2007 by Grosset & Dunlap. All rights reserved. Published
by Grosset & Dunlap, a division of Penguin Young Readers Group, 345 Hudson
Street, New York, New York 10014. GROSSET & DUNLAP is a trademark of
Penguin Group (USA) Inc. Printed in the U.S.A.

Library of Congress Control Number: 2006027929

ISBN 978-0-448-44451-2   10 9 8 7 6 5 4 3 2 1

camp CONFIDENTIAL

A Fair to Remember

by Melissa J. Morgan

Grosset & Dunlap

PROLOGUE

Posted by: Jenna
Subject: Memorial Day fun!!!

Hey there, peeps of 4A and 4C, have I got
a surprise for you! This Memorial Day weekend my
father has offered to take us all up to the lake house
so we can pig out, stay up all night talking, work on
our base tans, and make up for lost reunion time.

Ladies . . . pack your bags!

I mean, even though the reunion weekend
turned out all right in the end, we *were* split up.
And that, we all agreed, was no good. I think it's
about time we get the girls back together for a little
two-bunk bonding, don't you? Plus, Memorial Day
at the lake is out of control. They do this whole old-
fashioned, weekend-long, picnic/carnival thing
with tons of food and rides and tons of food and
shows and tons of food and fireworks.

Did I mention the *tons of food*?

(You know how much I love my stomach.)

Anyway, the point is, you are all invited and
I hope to see each and every one of you there. And

for those of you who are wondering (and I know you're out there), no, this is not one of my practical jokes. I can see why you would think so, but I'd never joke about a thing like this. I am perfectly and totally serious. But if you really need to confirm, you can have your parents call my dad. He's totally willing to answer their questions.

So pack your bags, ladies! It's time to have the *real* reunion we've all been waiting for! Can't wait to see you!!!

chapter ONE

"Bathing suit . . . check!" Jenna Bloom sang to herself as she shoved her one-piece into her duffel bag. "Greenwood Lake sweatshirt . . . check! Baseball cap . . . check!"

She yanked open the drawer to her bedside table and considered her stash of practical joke paraphernalia. Should she bring the whoopee cushion? The foaming mouth gum? The skin cream that looked like it was from some chichi makeup counter, but in fact turned your skin green? That could be fairly hilarious if she could convince Tori or Natalie that it was the latest in makeup technology from France or whatever.

But no. This weekend was not about pranks. It was about bonding with her friends. Being a "gracious hostess," as her mother had told her ten thousand times. And she had a feeling that Martha Stewart had never purposely turned her guests' faces green. With a deep breath and some serious willpower, Jenna slammed the drawer shut. No pranks this weekend. This Memorial Day was going to be about good clean fun.

"Jenna! Are you ready yet?" her mother called up the stairs. "Your father is going to be here any minute!"

"I'm trying, Mom!" Jenna shouted back, shoving her flip-flops into the bag. "But this packing thing is complicated."

"Your brother was done an hour ago!" her mom called. "It's just three days!"

Jenna rolled her eyes and yanked her bag off the bed. It dropped to the floor with a thump. How could Adam have been done an hour ago? They had just gotten home from school around that time. It had taken Jenna a half hour just to locate her duffel bag and find herself three T-shirts that weren't covered in wrinkles.

But it made sense that her twin brother was all ready to go. That was just the way he was. What Jenna couldn't figure out was *why* he wanted to go *at all*. Did he really want to spend the entire weekend in a house full of girls? How could that possibly be fun for him?

"Well, at least we'll outnumber him eight to one," Jenna said with a smirk, dropping down in front of her computer.

She had saved all the response e-mails from the friends who were coming to the lake and put them in their own little folder. On the list were Alex, Natalie, Grace, Brynn, Tori, Alyssa, and Valerie. Definitely a fun group. Jenna could not wait to see them all. She only wished that Sarah had agreed to come, but she had e-mailed a few days ago to decline. Apparently she had a big softball game that weekend that she just couldn't miss. Jenna understood that, being a sports fiend herself.

Plus this was Sarah's first year on her school team. She had tried out and made it after Abby, another camp friend who also went to Sarah's school, had talked her into it. Jenna was happy that Sarah was finally using her sick softball skills somewhere other than camp, but Sarah was going to be missed this weekend.

"Jenna! Please finish up and come down!" Jenna's mother shouted. "Your father is going to want to hit the road as soon as he gets here."

"Just have to shut down my computer, Mom!" Jenna yelled back.

She quickly typed up an e-mail to Sarah.

To: SarahSports
From: Aries8
Subject: The Big Game

Hi, Sarah!

Just wanted to wish you luck on your softball game this weekend! We'll be rooting for you from Greenwood Lake. Wish you could be there! We'll miss you!!!

Love,
Jenna

Jenna quickly logged off and shut down her computer. She heard her father's car pull up outside and her heart started to pound with excitement. This was it! The weekend was about to begin. In just a couple of hours, she would be hanging out with all her friends.

With some effort, Jenna hoisted her heavy bag from the floor and struggled through the door with it.

She shut off her bedroom light and clambered down the stairs.

"He's here! He's here! He's here!" she cheered, jumping down the last few steps.

Her feet hit at an odd angle and she tripped forward, taking out a potted plant with her bag and tripping right into someone's chest.

"Easy there, killer," the victim said, steadying Jenna with his hands on her arms.

Okay. That was not a member of her family. Jenna stood up straight and looked right into the light green eyes of David Carson. David, Adam's friend from camp. David, Sarah's *boyfriend.* Jenna's heart took a nose-dive and she stepped back. Practically *jumped* back.

"What are *you* doing here?" she blurted.

"Good to see you, too," David said with a smile. His floppy brown hair had been cut so that it didn't flop *completely* over his eye anymore. It just sort of grazed his eyebrow. "And you're welcome."

"For what?" Jenna asked.

"For catching you," he said.

"I was fine, thanks," Jenna said, straightening her T-shirt.

"Yeah. Tell that to the wallpaper that almost rearranged your face," Adam said from behind her. "And David is here because Dad said I could bring a friend this weekend. You know, because you've got, like, four *thousand* of them coming."

Jenna whirled on her brother, whose curly brown hair—so much like her own—was matted down by a Yankees baseball cap. "Maybe that's because this whole thing was *my* idea. You should have told me you were bringing someone."

"Why? So you could stick itching powder in his bed or something?" Adam asked, glancing out the window. He lifted his backpack as their dad started up the front walk. "I don't think so."

"No. I just, this whole weekend was my idea and . . . and . . . I would have wanted to know, that's all," Jenna said awkwardly, crossing her skinny arms over her chest.

"Well, now you do!" David told her with a smile.

Jenna narrowed her eyes at him. She just could not believe this was happening. Not just one boy on her perfect reunion weekend, but *two*. And why did it have to be *this* boy? The only boy she had ever had a crush on? A totally humiliating crush that only ended when Jenna found out that Sarah liked him and that he liked Sarah back. The two of them had danced together all night at the camp social while Jenna had looked on and tried not to be jealous. Now he was here and Sarah was not, and the whole thing was just making her feel all hot in the face.

The doorbell rang and Adam rushed to respond. There stood Jenna's dad, a huge smile on, his sunglasses perched atop his head.

"Everyone ready for a fun weekend?" he asked, spreading his arms wide.

"Yeah!" Adam and David cheered.

Jenna yanked her bag up off the tile floor and sighed, following after the boy brigade. So much for her perfect weekend.

△ △ △

Grace sat at the breakfast bar in her kitchen on Friday afternoon, eating her daily snack and staring at her history textbook. She knew that she should be excited about her weekend at Greenwood Lake with her friends, but somehow she just could not get psyched with that big, ugly book laughing up at her. She took a sip of her milk and let out a huge, dramatic sigh.

"Something wrong, Grace?" her mother asked, turning off the water in the kitchen sink. She wiped her hands on a towel and walked over. "Shouldn't you be bouncing off the walls about now? Alyssa and her mom are going to be here to pick you up any second now."

"I know," Grace said, tucking a stray lock of curly red hair behind her ear. "It's just . . . do I really have to bring . . . *that?*" she asked, throwing her hand out toward the thick book.

"Grace," her mother said in her stern, warning tone. "We've been over this and over this."

"I know," Grace said. "It's just that this weekend is supposed to be fun. How am I going to have any fun if I have to study?"

Her mother stood up straight and sighed. She looked, as always, perfectly put together in a pair of light khakis and a plaid, button-down shirt. Grace wondered if she'd ever look that perfect and pressed in her life.

"The only reason we're letting you go on this trip is because we have a deal. Don't tell me you're trying to back out of it. Because if you want to stay home . . ."

"No!" Grace blurted, suddenly on high alert. "No! I'll make good on the deal. Two hours of studying each day."

"Exactly," her mother said with a smile. "We only want you to pass that test on Tuesday. Because if you don't pass the test, you might not pass history for the year. And if you don't pass history for the year . . ."

"I know. I know. Summer school," Grace said, feeling heavy.

"And if you have to go to summer school . . ."

"It means I'll have to miss camp," Grace finished. And that would be a nightmare. It would basically be the punishment to end all punishments. Grace could *not* miss out on camp. She only looked forward to it all year long, from the moment she left her bunk for the last time in August until the moment she got back on the bus at the end of June. There was no way she could stay home from camp and study history instead.

Grace knew that she had brought this upon herself. It was just that every time she had gone to open her history textbook, something more important—and interesting—had seemed to come up. Like IMs from her camp friends, or practice for the school play, or some great soap opera marathon on cable. She had just always thought she would have the time to catch up, but now time had basically run out.

"At least it's only your history book," her mother said. "I could reconsider our deal and add your English book, too . . ."

"Just the history book is enough! My English test isn't for another whole week. Don't you think it's totally unfair to give a huge test the *day* after Memorial Day weekend?" Grace asked, getting up to put the bag of chocolate chip cookies back in the cupboard. "Come on, Mom. Even you have to admit that's evil."

Grace's mother hid a laugh behind her hand.

"Doesn't Mr. Joseph know that people have *lives?*" Grace added, throwing her hands out, hamming it up.

Her mother shook her head and smiled. "I'm sure your friends won't mind letting you alone for a few hours here and there this weekend," she said. "After all, they've always helped you study in the past. Like that summer when you had to catch up on your reading."

Grace smiled. "Yeah. They were really great about that."

A horn tooted in the driveway and Grace's excitement finally kicked in. "They're here!" she cried, grabbing her mini-suitcase and sleeping bag off the floor. "Bye, Mom!" she said, jumping up on her tiptoes to kiss her mother's cheek. She turned and ran for the door, yanking her denim jacket from the hook in the hallway along the way.

"Ahem!" her mother said loudly.

Grace stopped in her tracks and turned around. Her mom was standing a few feet behind her, holding her history textbook up in one hand. Grace blushed.

"Oops! Don't know how I forgot that!" she joked, tromping back to her mother. She took the book in one arm and almost fell over from its weight. "That's only the most important thing for me to bring with me!" she said.

"Uh-huh," her mother said with a smirk. She

leaned down and kissed Grace on top of her curls. "Have fun, honey. And study hard!"

"I will!" Grace said, running for the door again.

She rushed outside, closed the door behind her, and lifted her sleeping bag to wave awkwardly at the car. Alyssa waved back excitedly before jumping out of the backseat to help Grace with her things. Grace tucked her history book under her jacket as her friend ran up to her. The last thing she wanted to do was explain its presence to Alyssa. She wanted to forget all about the thing—for now.

"Hey, Grace!" Alyssa cried.

"Hey yourself!"

Alyssa looked amazing. She had cut her long black hair to just below her shoulders and had one small braid worked into the front with a colorful ribbon woven through it. She wore a beaded tank top and a long denim skirt, and her flip-flops had hand-painted flowers all over them.

"It's so good to see you!" Alyssa said, grabbing Grace up in a hug. Grace dropped her sleeping bag, and the book, of course, stabbed right through her jacket and into Alyssa's stomach. "Ow," she said, rubbing her tummy. "What was that?"

"Oh, nothing," Grace said. "Just a little light reading."

Alyssa looked at Grace like she was nuts, but didn't question her. "Let me get your bag. I'm dying to get up there already! We've been on the road ever since school let out. Sometimes I think South Jersey is just too far from everything."

"Except the shore," Grace pointed out.

Alyssa grinned. "Yes. I *love* that."

Grace smiled and picked up her sleeping bag again before following Alyssa back to her mom's station wagon. The book felt as if it was burning a hole through her New Jersey Devils T-shirt. She just couldn't imagine three whole days at Greenwood Lake with this thing taunting her the whole time, reminding her of what was at stake. Maybe she could "accidentally" drop it out the window somewhere along the drive.

Then she could actually have some fun this weekend.

chapter

TWO

Jenna jumped out of the front seat of her dad's car practically before it had come to a stop. All she could think about was getting away from Adam and David already. During the entire long drive to the lake, they had played every car game from "I Spy" to "Would You Rather?" and they hadn't let Jenna take part in any of them. Boys were so irritating. What she really needed right about now was some quality time with the girls.

Luckily, a few of them were already there, ready and waiting. Natalie's mother's SUV was sitting in the wide driveway and as soon as Jenna stepped around the back of the car she spotted her friends. Natalie, Alex, Valerie, and Brynn roused themselves from the rocking chairs on the wide porch of the house.

"You're here!" Jenna cried, running up the wood steps to meet them.

"*You're* here!" Brynn cried back. She threw her arms wide and Jenna crashed right into her, nearly knocking her off her feet. Then Natalie threw her arms around the both of them and soon all five girls were wrapped up in one giddy group hug.

Natalie's mother laughed. "Hello, Jenna," she said.

"Hi, Mrs. Goode!" Jenna replied.

As soon as Nat's mother had moved off to talk to Jenna's dad, Jenna let out a happy squeal. "You guys have *no* idea how good it is to see you," she said, elated.

"It's amazing just to be here," Natalie said, pushing her stylish sunglasses up into her dark hair. "Jenna, this place is incredible. Your house is just steps from the lake. Very posh."

"Eh, this old place?" Jenna said, beaming nevertheless.

A compliment from Natalie was like a compliment from the editor of *Vogue*. Having grown up in Manhattan with an art-dealer mother and a world-famous actor for a dad, Natalie was pretty much the last word on what was cool.

"I can't wait to see inside," Valerie said, her dark skin glowing with excitement. She was already decked out for the patriotic occasion in an American flag T-shirt and denim shorts. She even had red, white, and blue beads at the ends of all her tiny braids. "Are we all staying in the same room?"

"Yep. We have the big guest room," Jenna said. "They get the small one," she added, gesturing over her shoulder to where the boys were helping her father unpack the car.

Suddenly Alex's jaw dropped. "Adam is here?"

"Ooooooh!" Natalie, Val, and Brynn all teased.

"The couple of the century reunites!" Natalie added.

"Come on, you guys. We are *not* the couple of the century," Alex said, clearly embarrassed.

Jenna had to force herself not to roll her eyes. How had she spaced on the fact that her brother and Alex were in like? Now they were going to have to spend the whole weekend listening to ooey-gooey couple talk. Maybe it was a good thing Sarah hadn't come along. If she had, there would be *two* couples to deal with.

"Anyone heard from Grace and Alyssa? Or Tori?" Jenna asked, hoping to change the subject.

"Yes! Grace just called from her cell a little while ago. They're about an hour away," Brynn said.

"And Tori's flight gets in tonight," Natalie added. Tori was coming all the way from Los Angeles to join the festivities. "Her dad got her a driver, so she'll be here around dinnertime."

"Cool," Jenna said. She couldn't wait until everyone was here. It was going to be awesome to have the group together again.

"Natalie! I'm going!" Nat's mother called. "Come over and give me a hug."

"Oh, Mom," Natalie said, rolling her eyes. Still, she walked over to her mother's SUV and wrapped her arms around her.

"Omigosh. Here they come!" Brynn said under her breath, clutching Alex's arm. Sure enough, Adam, David, and Mr. Bloom were all on their way over. The guys clutched their bags and sleeping bags, and Mr. Bloom carried a big cooler.

"You guys! Don't make a big deal!" Alex said

through her teeth, although she was pretty much beaming with joy at the sight of Adam.

Ugh. That's my brother, Jenna thought. *She's all psyched over my dorky brother!*

"Hi, Adam," Alex said shyly as soon as Adam made it up the stairs.

"Hi, Alex," he said, his face all blotchy.

Then they just stood there and stared at each other. The giddy tension in the air was so thick, the hair on Jenna's arms stood up.

"Hi, everyone!" Mr. Bloom said, bringing up the rear. "Hope you haven't been waiting too long."

"Just a few minutes, Mr. Bloom," Brynn offered.

Alex took a deep breath. "So, Adam—"

"Hey, David," Adam said, turning to his friend. "Wanna go check out the lake?"

"Totally!" David said.

They dropped their stuff on the porch, then turned and sprinted off like their lives depended on it.

"Don't worry about us! We can bring everything inside!" Jenna's dad shouted after them.

Jenna and the other girls all looked at Alex, whose face had completely crumbled. Jenna felt like she could throttle her brother. How could he be so rude? Already this whole boy-girl thing was turning out to be a big mistake.

▲ ▲ ▲

"This room is *huge!*" Brynn said, walking into the guest room and dropping her bags on one of the throw rugs.

Alex followed Brynn and placed her things down next to hers. Valerie, Natalie, and Brynn rushed around the room, checking out the two double beds, the closet, and the attached bathroom. Alex wished that she could share their enthusiasm, but at the moment she was just feeling confused. At first she'd had no idea that Adam was going to be there. Then she'd seen him and gotten all excited, and then he'd totally blown her off. She'd gone from fine to psyched to blah in about five minutes. That could really throw a girl off.

"Alex! Check out the view!" Brynn said, leaning one knee on the window seat.

Trying to get in the spirit, Alex joined her friend and looked out. The immense bay window had an incredible view of the lake and the trees and the mountains beyond. Alex took a deep breath and sat down, gazing out at all the wondrous nature.

"You all right?" Natalie asked, wandering over. She sat down next to Alex on the cushion and smoothed her pink flowered skirt over her knees.

"I don't get it," Alex confessed. "It seemed like Adam didn't even want to see me."

"No. He totally did. Didn't you see the look on his face when you first said hi?" Natalie reminded her.

"Yeah," Alex said with a small smile. "But then why did he run off? We haven't seen each other in months."

"Listen, I have totally been there," Natalie said. "You know that disastrous date I had with Simon in Mystic? I looked forward to that forever and it turned out to be nothing like what I expected."

Alex's stomach turned. "Right. And then you guys broke up," she said, alarmed. "Are you saying that Adam and I are going to break up?"

Natalie's eyes widened in panic. "No! No! Not at all. Just . . . try not to expect too much from him. Give him the benefit of the doubt. After all, he *is* a boy."

"And boys are totally weird," Brynn put in.

"I'll second that!" Jenna exclaimed, bounding over.

"Me too!" Valerie put in.

"Remember that time Kyle from my school told everyone we were dating when we *so* weren't?" Natalie said.

"That was nothing. You should have heard David in the car just now. His 'Would You Rathers' were completely gross," Jenna said. "I don't know how Sarah puts up with him. He is just *so* immature."

"I thought you *liked* gross stuff," Alex said, confused.

"Oh yeah. That's right," Jenna said, blushing slightly. "But still. The point is, boys are weird. *Especially* my brother."

Alex smiled. "Thanks, guys. You're right. I should just chill out."

"Exactly! Chill out and have some fun," Natalie said. "That's what this weekend is all about, right?"

"Right!" the others agreed.

Natalie gave Alex a quick hug, then jumped up to unpack. Alex saw something move out of the corner of her eye and her heart caught when she saw Adam and David down at the lake, throwing rocks into the clear water. She liked Adam so much. What if he wasn't just being a weird boy? What if he didn't like her anymore?

Suddenly the door to the guest room was flung open and in stepped Grace and Alyssa.

"Let's get this party started!" Grace shouted, throwing her arms wide.

Alex laughed. Sometimes when Grace was around, she just couldn't *not* laugh.

"Hey, guys!" Jenna cried as everyone jumped up for more hugs.

"All right! Which bed is mine?" Grace asked.

"Oh, no! You guys got here late so you get the floor tonight," Brynn told her. "Tomorrow we switch."

"Fine by me," Grace said.

She whipped her sleeping bag out and laid it on the floor between the beds. Then she dropped her suitcase on it followed by a book. A big, fat book that landed with a thud.

"*What* is *that?*" Valerie asked.

"That is my evil history teacher's idea of a joke," Grace said, sitting down next to the book. "I may as well tell you guys the bad news now. I have to study this weekend."

"I knew something was up!" Alyssa said. "A girl just does not bring a book that heavy with her on a vacation weekend unless there's a good reason."

"You're kidding," Alex said. "You have to study?"

"Yep. I have a huge history test on Tuesday and if I don't pass, I won't be at Camp Lakeview this summer," Grace said. "I'll be in . . ." She paused to swallow and make a disgusted face. "Summer school."

"No!" all the girls cried at once.

"And my school doesn't even have air-conditioning!" Grace grumbled.

"In that case, we will totally help you study," Brynn said, sitting down next to Grace. "We've all seen what happens to your hair in the humidity."

"Ha-ha," Grace said, but smiled.

"We'll totally help. Whatever we can do, Grace," Valerie put in, slinging her arm over Grace's shoulders.

"Camp Lakeview would not be Camp Lakeview without you," Alex added.

Grace grinned up at her. "Thanks, you guys. But let's not think about this right now," she added, shoving the book under her sleeping bag. She jumped up and threw her arms over her head. "Let's party 4A/4C style!"

Natalie turned on the stereo on top of the dresser and suddenly everyone was dancing and whooping and singing. Soon enough, Alex was having so much fun that she forgot all about Adam and his weirdness. For now.

▲ ▲ ▲

"Tori, I love your pj's!" Valerie said as Tori walked out of the bathroom later that night. "Where did you get those?"

Tori looked down at her silk shorts and top, which were covered in cartoon cupcakes. She tied her long blonde hair atop her head and smiled.

"They're cute, right? I got them at this new shop

on Rodeo. Iphegenia was there buying the *same* ones," she said, her blue eyes shining.

"Iphegenia?" Grace squealed. "I heard she just had her legs insured for fifty million dollars."

"You have the life, Tori," Brynn said, leaning back with one of her celebrity magazines.

"Whatever. I just wish I didn't live so far away from all you guys," Tori said, sitting down and slipping her feet into her sleeping bag. She grabbed a handful of popcorn out of the big bowl Jenna had brought up and popped a kernel into her mouth. "I love California, but that plane ride is *not* fun."

"Speaking of fun," Jenna said, whipping out a sheet of blue paper. "My dad gave me the schedule for the weekend events."

"Cool!" Valerie said, grabbing the paper from Jenna's fingers. "Let's see what's going on around here."

Tori and Natalie gathered around Val as they read over the list of events. Val's eyes took in phrases like "dance in the gazebo," "finger-lickin' barbecue," "potato-sack race," and "face painting." When Jenna had told them this was going to be an old-fashioned good time, she hadn't been kidding.

"Hey, Jenna. What's this?" Alyssa asked, stepping out of the bathroom with a black box in her hand.

Jenna hopped off the end of her bed to check it out. "Omigosh! I can't believe that's still in there!" she exclaimed, her eyes widening.

"What is it?" Val asked, curious.

"Blue hair dye," Jenna said, holding the box up. "I bought it when I was about ten and my mom and I were fighting about my haircut. I wanted to cut it short and my mom didn't want me to, so I rode my bike to the drugstore in town and bought this with my allowance. Once I threatened to dye my hair blue if she wouldn't let me cut it, she gave in."

"I totally remember that haircut!" Alex exclaimed. "You looked like a Muppet!"

As the longest campers at Camp Lakeview, Alex and Jenna had been together through almost everything. Including plenty of bad hair.

"Alex!" Grace scolded as everyone laughed.

"No! She's right. I did," Jenna said. "Now I always listen to my mom when it comes to my hair." She looked at Alyssa. "Do you want to use it?"

Alyssa had a long history of experimenting with her hair and its color.

"Maybe. It could be cool," Alyssa said with a shrug, pulling some of her hair in front of her face to inspect it. "You know, get in the patriotic spirit. But I think I still need to think about it," she added, placing the box back in the bathroom.

Valerie returned her attention to the schedule and her eyes suddenly fell on something intriguing.

"Check it out, you guys! There's a talent contest on Monday afternoon!" she announced, holding the page up.

"No way!" Grace said.

"Cool! We have to do it!" Brynn added.

Grace and Brynn were the two actresses of the group. They never turned down an opportunity to get up onstage.

"Maybe I could choreograph a dance for us!" Valerie suggested, excited. She had been taking dance lessons this past year and was getting really good at it. "How cool would that be?"

"Oh, we would so win," Tori said. "Who could resist eight gorgeous girls dancing?" she added, batting her eyelashes.

Everyone laughed. Jenna stood up, popping a piece of popcorn into her mouth. "I'll do it, but only if you guys don't mind me crushing all your toes."

"Jenna! You are not a bad dancer," Natalie protested.

"Wanna bet?" Jenna said. "Turn on the music."

Grace was closest to the stereo, so she cranked it up. Instantly Jenna started dancing around, throwing her arms out off beat and totally playing around. She looked like a confused chicken, jutting her hips all over the place and wagging her head around. Valerie was pretty much rolling on the floor with laughter after about two minutes. As was everyone else.

Then the door flew open and Adam and David jumped in armed with cans of Silly String.

"Ambush!" they shouted at the top of their lungs.

Natalie screamed and ducked for cover, but everyone else was too taken off guard. Suddenly Adam and David unleashed a Silly String attack, running all around the room and dousing everyone with the sticky stuff.

"Stop! Stop!" Grace cried, shielding her hair.

"Get out, you freaks!" Jenna shouted.

"Get them!" Valerie yelled.

She grabbed a pillow and started fighting back, even though she could barely see through all the string. Tori, Brynn, and Grace jumped up to help, using their own pillows to battle back. Soon the guys were out of string and the room was completely covered. All eight girls descended upon them with pillows and they were forced to retreat. Jenna slammed the door on them the second they were out in the hall.

"We so got you!" David shouted.

"Take that!" Adam added.

Valerie, Jenna, and the others turned around to survey the damage. There wasn't a blanket, sleeping bag, or piece of furniture left un-stringed. The girls were going to have a lot of cleaning up to do.

"Stupid boys," Jenna grumbled.

THREE

"Would you rather . . . stand on your head for an hour or . . . eat an ice cream sundae with anchovies?" Tori asked Jenna as they made their way onto the fairgrounds on Saturday morning. They had gathered up a bunch of blankets and snacks in their backpacks, along with magazines, half a dozen pots of nail polish, and a Frisbee—everything eight girls needed to entertain themselves during a sunny day in the park.

"Ice cream with anchovies, definitely," Jenna said.

"Eww!" her friends all cried.

"You will eat *anything!*" Brynn said, sticking her tongue out.

"What? If you stand on your head that long, your brain explodes!" Jenna told them. "It's, like, a scientific fact."

"I don't know about that," Alyssa said with a smile. "But your face would probably be red for a *very* long time."

Jenna laughed. Playing "Would You Rather" with her friends was *so* much better than playing it with Adam and David.

"How about, would you rather stand on your head for an hour or take a huge history test the day after Memorial Day weekend?" Grace said grumpily, looking down at the textbook she was holding to her chest.

"Take a huge history test!" Valerie told her, slinging her arm around Grace's shoulders. "Especially when you have all of us to help you study."

Grace brightened a bit as the girls came to the makeshift fence surrounding the carnival area.

"Check it out!" Jenna cried, racing forward.

Behind the fence, a troop of big, burly men were setting up a dozen cool-looking rides. There was a Sidewinder, a Tilt-A-Whirl, a Gravitron, a Ferris wheel, and tons of other colorful rides that hadn't been put together yet. Plus there were tons of games, like a dunking booth and a dart-and-balloon game with huge stuffed animals hanging from their rafters, just waiting to be won. But what really got Jenna's attention were the food stands. Cotton candy, hot dogs, deep-fried Oreos, ice cream, pretzels. Everything a girl could ever want to eat. Jenna spotted a woman behind a counter dipping apples in caramel sauce. Jenna actually licked her lips. Those apples looked like heaven.

"I'm so going on that one!" Grace said, pointing at the Gravitron.

"If you go on that and don't barf, I'll give you a million dollars," Valerie told her.

Grace shoved her hand out. "Deal."

"Hey! When do the rides start up?" Jenna shouted to the man closest to the fence.

He scratched at his sizable belly and looked up at the sun. "'Round six o'clock. Come back then and we should be good to go."

"Cool!" Jenna cheered.

"Come on, you guys," Natalie said. "Let's check out the rest of the fairgrounds."

As the girls walked around the fence, they saw tons of families setting up picnic blankets for lunch. Kids ran around with balloons tied to their wrists and a few clowns circulated the crowd, doing magic tricks and making balloon animals. A bunch of high-school guys were playing a game of tag football in the center of a huge field, and big band music was being piped over hidden speakers.

"This really is a big, old-fashioned party," Brynn said, her eyes wide.

Jenna spotted a banner that read OLDE-TYME BLUE RIBBON COMPETITION. It hung over a table with a short line in front of it, where a woman seemed to be signing people up for something.

"What's that about?" Jenna asked.

"Oh! I saw that on the schedule," Valerie said. "It sounded like fun."

"Let's check it out!" Jenna suggested.

Once again, Jenna raced ahead and all of her friends laughed and jogged to catch up with her. Jenna knew she was acting like a crazed puppy, but she didn't want to miss anything.

"Hi!" Jenna said to the middle-aged woman behind the table. She was wearing a blue T-shirt, a red jacket, and a red, white, and blue ribbon that read

Olde-Tyme Committee. "Can you tell us about the competition?" Jenna asked.

Alex fell in next to Jenna and the rest of their friends gathered around, some of them out of breath.

"Sure!" the woman said with a smile. "We'll be holding several events over the course of the weekend," she said, handing over an information sheet. "How old are you girls?"

"Thirteen," Alex answered, sounding proud.

"All righty. We have a three-legged race, a wheelbarrow race, and a balloon toss in your age division," the woman said, quickly consulting her clipboard. "In each event you earn points for coming in first, second, or third, and the pair with the most points at the end of the weekend wins."

"What do you win?" Tori asked, slipping to the front of the group.

"A ribbon and a trophy," the woman told her.

"Sounds great," Jenna said.

"Good! All you need is a partner and you can sign up," the woman told her.

Jenna looked at Alex. The two of them were known for being the most athletic girls in their division at Camp Lakeview.

"What do you think?" Jenna asked.

"I think we can take anyone," Alex replied with a grin, high-fiving Jenna.

The woman's face fell. "Oh, I'm sorry, hon," she said. "But your partner has to be a boy."

"What?" Jenna blurted.

"Well, one of the rules is that all pairs be boy-girl," the woman told her with a shrug. "That way it keeps the competition even."

"No fair!" Alex cried. "Jenna and I can compete against any all-boy team."

"And win!" Jenna added.

"Yeah!" the other girls cheered.

"Well, now, ladies. I didn't say it was to keep it fair for the *girls*," the woman said with a mischievous glint in her eyes.

Slowly, Jenna smiled. She liked this lady. But that didn't change the fact that she wasn't going to let her and Alex sign up. Shoulders slumping, Jenna turned away from the table.

"This stinks," she said, trudging away.

Her friends gathered in around her. "No doubt," Valerie said.

Jenna really wanted to join that competition. She loved those kinds of silly, fun events. But even more so, she *loved* to compete. And win. If she wanted to sign up with one of her friends and have some good, olde-tyme fun, they should have let her.

Why did it seem like the whole world was trying to force her to hang out with boys?

▲ ▲ ▲

"Hey, you guys! Look!" Valerie said, pointing across the huge main field. "They're setting up a stage over there."

"That must be where the talent competition is gonna happen," Brynn said, lifting her sunglasses off her eyes for a moment. "Let's go sign up!" Valerie led the girls as they wove their way around picnicking families, ball-chasing dogs, and a bunch of kids fighting over who got to fly their kite next. By the time they reached the big, whitewashed stage, they were practically skipping. Valerie couldn't wait to sign up for the show and get started on their routine. She just hoped there weren't any surprise rules in store, like there had been for Jenna's competition. If she had to work boys into her dance number, she was out.

A woman with a blonde ponytail stood atop a tall ladder, twisting a bulb into one of the light fixtures above the stage. Valerie climbed the steps to the platform and looked up at her, shielding her eyes with her hand to block out the sun.

"Excuse me?" she said. "Is this where we sign up for the talent contest?"

"Sure is!" the woman replied with a smile. "Just head backstage and see Mr. Cox. He'll get you all set up."

"Thanks!" Valerie told her. She turned to her friends. "We have to go back—"

But Brynn and Grace were already halfway there, the others trailing behind them. Valerie grinned and rolled her eyes. Apparently her friends were just as excited about this as she was.

"Hey! Wait up!" she called out, jogging to catch them. She wanted to be the one to talk to this Mr. Cox guy. After all, signing up for the talent show had been *her* idea.

But when she got behind the curtain, she realized she shouldn't have worried. All of her friends were gathered around three huge racks of costumes, oohing and aahing over the sequins and beads.

"Look at this!"

Natalie slipped a pink feather boa off a hanger and tossed it around her neck, striking a pose. Grace grabbed a top hat and placed it on her head.

"You're looking *mah*-velous this evening, madame!" she said to Natalie with a bow.

"Well thank you, I'm sure!" Natalie said back in a breathless voice.

"Wow, you guys are easily distracted," Valerie said, putting her hands on her hips. "We're supposed to be signing up for the show, remember?"

"Did I hear someone say they wanted to sign up for my show?"

Valerie turned around and looked into the dark brown eyes of a very good-looking, college-aged guy in a white T-shirt and jeans. He had short brown hair gelled up into little peaks all over his head and tanned skin. He was so cute he could have been a model.

It was too bad Becky, Valerie's counselor from bunk 4C, wasn't there with them. She would have been flirting like crazy with this guy right off the bat.

"Are you Mr. Cox?" Valerie asked.

He cracked a grin. "Call me Greg," he said. He looked from Valerie to her friends behind her and smirked as he picked up a clipboard from a nearby table. "So what's your talent? Trying on all my costumes?"

Instantly the girls scrambled to return all the stuff to where it had been. Greg laughed. "No! It's okay, it's okay. No harm done."

"Actually, we're a dance troupe," Valerie told him, going for a mature, no-nonsense expression.

Behind her, Valerie's friends knocked over the hat rack with a crash. Greg winced, but said nothing.

"A dance troupe, huh?" he said. "I'm a dancer myself. Hip-hop, mostly. What's your style?"

We don't have one . . . yet, Valerie thought. But she couldn't tell him that. If he knew they didn't actually *have* a style or a routine, he might not want them in his show.

"Oh, uh . . . it's kind of a modern, hip-hop, African fusion thing," Valerie blundered, thinking back to her dance classes at home.

Greg's face lit up. "Wow! Sounds amazing. We've never had a full dance troupe before."

"Really?" Valerie said with a grin. "Well then you're gonna *love* us."

"I'm sure I will," Greg said. "What's your name?"

"Valerie Williams," she said. "Why?"

"So I can sign you up," Greg said, making a note on his clipboard.

"Oh, right," Valerie said, embarrassed.

"Valerie Williams and dance troupe," he said. "I can't wait to see your routine."

"Yeah! Me neither!" Grace said, jumping up next to Valerie.

Greg's brow creased. "You don't have a routine yet? The competition is two days away."

Valerie felt her face burn. Here she was trying to look like a serious dancer/choreographer, and Grace was making her look like she had no idea what she was doing.

"No! Of course we have a routine!" Valerie said. "She's just kidding."

"All right then. Well, break a leg!" Greg said.

"Thanks!" Valerie told him.

The moment Greg was gone, Valerie turned to her friends. "All right. That's it. We have to go home and work on the routine. Like, now."

"Now?" Jenna asked. "But we brought all this stuff to hang out."

"So we'll hang out at home. And dance," Valerie said. "You heard Greg. The competition is two days away. I don't want to look like a complete moron in front of everyone."

"Okay," Jenna said with a shrug. "I'm kinda hungry anyway."

"Shocker," Tori teased. "I'm in!" she said, slipping her arm around Valerie's. "Let's go put on our dancing shoes!"

"But I didn't bring any dancing shoes," Jenna joked.

"Actually, you guys, I should probably study," Grace said, biting her lip. "Sorry, Val."

"That's okay," Valerie said, heading back out into the sun. "You study and we'll work on the routine and just teach you the steps later."

As the girls started back across the fairgrounds and headed for home, Valerie was already choreographing the routine in her head. The last thing she wanted was to look like some amateur in front of everyone at the fair. But as she looked around at her smiling, gabbing friends, she knew they would be all right. As long as they all worked together, they would come up with a show-stopping routine.

chapter

FOUR

"I love this music, Tori!" Valerie said, her head bopping to the beat coming through the portable CD player's speakers. "Who is this?"

"They're called Nova. They're this new band from London," Tori told her, dropping down on one of the cushy chairs on the Blooms' back deck. "My dad might be their U.S. representation."

Tori's dad was an entertainment lawyer in Los Angeles and had an inside track on everything that went on in Hollywood. Which meant that Tori was always up on who the next big actors and singers were going to be.

"Ooh! I like this part!" Brynn said, jumping up. "This would be a good place for a little spin move, right?"

Brynn whipped around and did a quick stutter step, then slid to the right.

"Sweet!" Valerie said, pushing herself out of her seat. She quickly rewound the CD to Brynn's part. Together they both did the move in exact unison. "I like it!" Valerie said, slapping hands with Brynn. "You guys! Check this out. We should all give it a try."

Tori got up and stood behind Valerie and Brynn, and then Natalie joined her. Jenna and Alex, however, were engaged in a serious thumb war and were too busy trying to knock each other out of their seats to notice. Alyssa, meanwhile, had her nose buried in a novel under the shade of the table umbrella.

"You guys! Come on!" Valerie said. "Don't you want to learn this? We have to have a killer routine by Monday."

Alyssa lowered her book. "Right! Sorry," she said. She placed her bookmark between the pages. "Where do you want me?"

"Why don't you stand behind us so you can copy the move?" Brynn suggested.

"Okay. Alex, Jenna? Earth to Alex and Jenna!" Alyssa teased as she walked by them.

Alex finally pinned Jenna's thumb, and Jenna groaned hugely. But at least their thumb war was over and they finally joined the others. Everyone fell into place behind Valerie and Brynn and waited for direction.

"Okay. Here's the move," Valerie said. "Five, six, seven, eight."

She and Brynn went through the eight-count move and Valerie described what she was doing as she did it. "Turn around, right foot in, step, step, and *slide!*"

"Nice!" Natalie said. "Let's all try." Tori reached over and restarted the music. Everyone began moving as one and Valerie grinned. They were getting it! Already they were on their way! But as soon as the spin was over, Jenna stepped left when she should have stepped right. Meanwhile, Alex missed the stutter step completely and just went right into her slide. Alyssa lost track of what she was doing and completely stopped, tripping herself, and Alex banged into her, sending them both into the railing around the deck. Only Tori and Natalie really got the move.

Valerie had a feeling she had a lot of work ahead of her.

"Oh! Oops!" Alex said, blushing.

"I completely spaced. Sorry," Alyssa told Val.

"It's no problem," Valerie said. "Let's just try it again."

Just then the sliding door to the house opened up and out walked Adam and David. Adam tossed a volleyball up and down as they approached. Everyone looked at Alex, who had pretty much lost all the color in her face.

"Hey, everyone! How's the dance party?" David joked.

"Fine. It's going great," Valerie answered.

"What do you guys want?" Jenna asked flatly. "We're trying to practice here, in case you hadn't noticed."

"Excuse us, Queen Jenna," Adam said, holding up one hand in surrender. "I just wanted to ask Alex something."

Alex eyed him nervously. "Yeah?"

"We're going down to the beach to bump the ball around," Adam said, popping the ball from hand to hand. "They have a net down there and everything. Wanna come?"

Alex's entire face instantly lit up. It was the first time Adam had talked directly to her all day. But then she seemed to remember that her friends were all watching.

"Actually, we're supposed to be working on this routine . . ." she said reluctantly.

"Oh, don't worry about it!" Natalie said, waving her off. "We'll be okay."

"Natalie!" Val said through her teeth.

"Valerie," Nat whispered. "She clearly wants to go. Give the girl a break."

"I'm no good at coming up with this stuff anyway, Val," Alex said hopefully. "Do you think maybe you guys can just teach me the steps later when you teach Grace?"

She had a point. Alex was a soccer star and a super athlete, but dancing was not one of her special talents. And besides, her eyes were practically begging. She really wanted to spend some time with Adam.

"Okay. That'll work," Valerie said finally. "You guys have fun."

"Thank you so much!" Alex said happily. "See ya!" Then she took off with the boys, barreling down the outside stairs.

"Who knew that Alex Kim could be so boy crazy?" Jenna grumbled.

"One day, Jenna, you are going to fall totally in love and then we are all so going to pick on you," Natalie said, wrapping her arm around Jenna's back.

"Yeah. You wish," Jenna shot back with a smile.

"Okay, you guys. Let's focus. We'll do the move again," Valerie said, reaching for the CD player. "On one. Ready?"

The backdoor slid open again. This time it was Grace and she did not look happy.

"You guys! I'm doomed!" she cried dramatically, throwing her hands out.

Instantly Alyssa and Jenna left the dance line. They ran over to Grace. "What's the matter?" Alyssa said.

"I cannot memorize dates!" Grace said, her eyes wide. "It's like I'm brain-dead or something. They just will not stay in there," she told them, knocking her head with the heel of her hand.

"It's okay. We'll help you!" Jenna offered, tugging Grace back toward the house.

"I have a great memorization game," Alyssa told her. "It always works for me."

"Really?" Grace said, brightening slightly. "You're the best!" Valerie felt herself growing frustrated as two more of her friends deserted her. But what was she going to do? Tell them not to help Grace? No way. Val wanted Grace to pass history and come back to Camp Lakeview this summer as much as the rest of them did. Grace's grades were a lot more important than Valerie's talent competition.

"Just come back as soon as you can!" she called after them.

"We will!" Jenna shouted, slamming the door behind her.

"And then there were four," Natalie joked.

"Huh?" Brynn said.

"Oh, it's just from this Agatha Christie book we read in English," Natalie said. "Never mind. Let's keep dancing."

"Okay. One more time!" Valerie said, hitting the play button.

At least she had been left with the three best dancers. Maybe together the four of them would be able to work out a good routine. She just hoped there would be time to teach everyone else later. Otherwise this talent competition would be over before Valerie ever got to the stage.

▲ ▲ ▲

"It just does not get any better than this!" Jenna said, dropping down at the picnic table her friends had snagged at the fairgrounds.

Her plastic plate was overflowing with two hot dogs, baked beans, corn on the cob, and potato chips. All around her, hundreds of people chatted and laughed and milled around, checking out the buffet-style barbecue. The entire town had turned out.

"How did I know that the 'finger-lickin' barbecue' would be Jenna's favorite thing on the schedule?" Valerie joked, placing the sheet of events on the table.

"I am just that predictable," Jenna said. She took a big bite of her overloaded hot dog and smiled in ecstasy.

"It's an amazing spread," Natalie said, sitting down with her big plastic bowl full of salad and grilled chicken. "There's something for everyone."

"I bet even Alex could find something good to eat," Tori said. "If we had any idea where she was."

Alex was diabetic and had a bunch of special dietary requirements. Jenna knew it was tough on her friend and was relieved that there were so many choices at the barbecue. But at the moment it didn't really matter since no one had seen Alex since she'd ditched them that morning for Jenna's brother.

"She might miss the whole thing if she doesn't get here soon," Brynn fretted, taking a sip of her lemonade.

"She's the one who wanted to hang out with the boys, so she'll just have to suffer the consequences," Jenna said, shrugging. "Knowing them, they probably tied her to a tree and left her there."

"Jenna!" Alyssa said, pausing with her corn on the cob halfway to her mouth. "Your brother would never do something like that to Alex."

"I was just kidding. Sheesh," Jenna said, rolling her eyes.

"Hey! There she is!" Grace announced, gesturing with her plastic fork.

Sure enough, Alex was bounding through the crowd, her dark hair flying, a huge smile on her face. Adam and David both brought up the rear, looking every bit as excited as Alex did.

"Hey, you guys!" Alex said, dropping down at the end of their table, the farthest seat from Jenna. "Guess what? Adam and I just signed up for the olde-tyme competition!"

Jenna's heart dropped. "You *did?*"

"Yep," Adam said, grabbing a potato chip off Jenna's plate. "And we're totally going to win, too."

Jenna dropped her hot dog and slumped on the picnic bench. She couldn't believe that both Alex and Adam were going to get to compete and she wasn't. Not that she wanted to spend the entire weekend with her twin, but shouldn't he have asked *her* to be his partner before asking Alex? Wasn't that what family was for?

"Hey, Jenna. Alex said you really wanted to sign up, too," David said. "Want to be my partner?"

Instantly the entire group fell silent. Everyone turned to stare at Jenna. She was just as surprised as they were.

"Huh?" she said.

"Yeah. There's still time," David said with a shrug. "The first event doesn't start for a couple of hours."

Jenna looked around at her friends, her heart fluttering nervously. David wanted to be her partner? Sarah's boyfriend? Her former crush? The very idea was making her palms clammy.

"Uh . . . what about Sarah?" Jenna asked, swallowing hard.

David raised his eyebrows. "What *about* Sarah?"

"Well, she *is* your girlfriend," Tori pointed out.

"So?" David said. "What does that have to do with anything?"

"Don't you think Sarah might mind?" Alyssa said. "You know, you partnering with another girl?"

Jenna couldn't have been more grateful for her friends just then. They were saying all the things she wanted to say, but couldn't seem to get out past the lump in her throat.

"You guys are kidding, right?" David said, looking around the table. "It's just a fun competition. And Sarah's not here. I bet if you called her right now she would tell us we should have signed up already. She wouldn't want us to miss out."

Jenna looked at Natalie across the table. Natalie was more experienced than anyone else at the table when it came to boy-girl matters. She and Simon had started being boyfriend and girlfriend way before Jenna even *thought* about having a crush. Natalie had even been through a breakup already. She was totally sophisticated.

"What do you think?" Jenna asked.

"I think he's right," Natalie said with a shrug. "Sarah would want you guys to have fun. It's really not a big deal."

This made Jenna feel slightly better, but her stomach still squirmed at the idea of spending so much of her weekend with David. Aside from her old crush on him, she had come here to hang out with her girls, not to hang out with a guy.

"I think you're just chicken," Adam said, stealing another chip. "You don't want to sign up because you know me and Alex are gonna whip you guys."

"You know it!" Alex said with a grin.

Instantly Jenna's competitive juices started flowing. She narrowed her eyes at Alex.

"You going to let them disrespect us like that?" David joked.

Jenna swung her legs over the end of the bench and stood up. "No way," she said, determined. "Come on, David. Let's go sign up."

"Wow. This is serious," Grace said as Jenna walked around the table. "You're really going to leave all that food behind?"

"That's what happens when someone challenges me," Jenna said with a grin. Then she looked at her brother, who was already eyeing her corn on the cob. "Just keep him away from it," she told her friends. "I'll be back."

Jenna's friends laughed as she and David headed off for the sign-up table. It looked like Jenna was going to get to compete after all. Thanks to a boy. It was strange the way things worked out.

chapter
FIVE

Jenna stood near the starting line for the three-legged competition, staring at the spectators to keep from staring at the top of David's head. He was down on the grass, tying his ankle to hers with the nylon rope he'd gotten from one of the olde-tyme committee members. For some reason, being so close to him was making her feel all twitchy. Like one loud noise would make her jump out of her skin. She finally spotted her friends in the crowd, right near the center of the makeshift course, and waved. They all waved back excitedly.

"Okay. That should do it," David said, standing. "You ready to run for your life?"

Jenna nodded. She looked down the straight, flat course, marked off at four corners by orange ribbons on stakes. A huge banner that read FINISH hung a couple hundred yards away. It looked like a really long way to run. Especially with one of her ankles tied to a boy's.

Next to them, Adam and Alex were already tied together and their heads were bent toward each other, talking strategy. Behind them, dozens of other pairs practiced walking around or pointed down the course, checking things out. The excitement in the air was making Jenna's heart pound. She really wanted to win this thing. Maybe she should concentrate on that instead of on the fact that David's leg was pressed right into hers.

"So . . . should we step with our tied feet first, or with our free feet?" she asked David.

"You pick," David told her, shoving his bangs back. "I'm putting you in charge."

"Me? Why?" Jenna asked.

"Because if I come up with a strategy and we lose, then you have seven friends to sic on me," he joked. "I've only got Adam, and don't tell him I said this, but I think you can take him."

Jenna laughed and instantly everything inside of her relaxed. "Oh, you're right about that," she said.

She had almost forgotten how cool and funny David could be. Maybe he was only an irritating boy when he was around Adam. It wouldn't surprise her. Adam was so annoying sometimes, she was sure he could infect anyone.

"Okay, let's start with our tied feet," Jenna said.

"Sounds like a plan," David said, rubbing his hands together. "Oh! Looks like we're about to start."

Sure enough, a chubby man in a red, white, and blue striped shirt was approaching a microphone on the platform near the finish line. He wore a white straw hat with a red, white, and blue striped ribbon around it.

"Attention all three-legged competitors!" he said

into the mic, his voice booming over the fairgrounds. "Please take your positions at the starting line!"

Nervous butterflies danced in Jenna's stomach. She and David made their way awkwardly to the white starting line painted on the grass. Jenna looked over at Adam, and he nodded at her with a serious expression. Jenna knew that look her brother was giving her. It was a "you're toast" kind of look.

"Oh, it's so on," Jenna said under her breath.

"Wow. You really *do* like to compete," David said.

"And win," Jenna told him.

"I'll have to remember that," David said.

"All right, everyone!" the man at the microphone called out. He lifted a starter pistol into the air. "On your mark! Get set! Go!"

The pistol went off and immediately Jenna started to run. Unfortunately, she took off with her free foot instead of her tied foot. Both of her legs went out from under her as David jerked her forward. Her stomach swooped and she started to go down. This was going to hurt.

"Watch it!" David shouted, grabbing her arm and hauling her back up. "I thought you said start with our tied feet!"

"Sorry!" Jenna cried. "Let's go!"

Everyone else already seemed to be ten yards ahead of them. Jenna and David stepped forward with their tied feet and started to move. Jenna focused with all her might on matching David's stride. Up ahead, a pair went down, falling head over heels. Then another hit the ground facefirst.

"We're gaining on them!" David cried.

"Faster!" Jenna shouted.

Alex and Adam were in the lead and she could not let them win. She and David got into a rhythm and were suddenly flying down the course. The crowd on either side of the course screamed and shouted and jumped up and down.

"Go, Jenna!" she heard Grace shout. "Go! Go! Go!"

All of a sudden, Alex and Adam tripped and hit the ground on their knees. The moment they did, Jenna and David blew right by them. The finish line was only ten feet away. Eight! Six! They were going to do it! "We have our winners!" the man cried into the microphone as David and Jenna stepped over the finish line ahead of everyone else.

"We did it!" Jenna cried.

"Woohoo!" David cheered. He grabbed her in a triumphant hug and Jenna threw her arms around him, laughing like crazy.

Wait a minute! What am I doing? Jenna thought, suddenly finding herself with her chin on David's shoulder. She instantly sprang back, but her ankle was still tied to David's. Her arms flailed for balance, but it was too late. This time, Jenna was going down.

David tried to grab her, but Jenna hit the ground on her butt—hard. She overheated with embarrassment as her friends all rushed toward her.

"Are you okay?" Alyssa cried, crouching next to her.

Grace dropped down to untie the rope around

Jenna and David's ankles.

"I'm . . . I'm fine," Jenna said, shaking her head. She tried really hard not to think about how ridiculous that fall must have looked. "We won!"

"Yeah, you did!" Valerie cheered, hugging her on the ground.

"Nice work," Adam said grudgingly, joining them.

Alex reached out her hands to Jenna and hauled her up off the grass. "You guys were great," she said with a smile.

"Thanks," Jenna said, blushing. She reached back to dust the dirt and grass off the butt of her denim shorts.

Suddenly the MC was breaking into their little group. "Here you go, kids! First-place ribbons!" he said, handing one blue ribbon to Jenna and one to David. "That's fifty points in the olde-tyme competition."

Everyone cheered. Then the MC turned to Alex and Adam. "And for you, third-place ribbons!" he said, producing yellow ribbons for them. "That's thirty-five points. You're all still in it! Congratulations!"

Alex and Adam took their ribbons and everyone cheered again. Then the MC moved off to award the second-place ribbons to another pair.

"We could actually win this thing!" David said, hanging his ribbon off one of the buttons on his polo shirt.

"Yeah," Jenna said, beaming as she admired her ribbon. Maybe competing with a boy wasn't so bad after all. "Yeah, we actually could."

"First *and* third place?" Jenna's father said that night as he and David set up a folding table at the end of the long dining room table. "My kids are very talented."

Alex glanced proudly at Adam as she sat down with a stack of napkins to fold, but he didn't look up from the chair he was placing.

"Yeah, we are," Jenna cheered. "But I'm *more* talented. I have the blue ribbon to prove it."

Adam scoffed. "Just wait till tomorrow. We're coming back."

"Definitely," Alex said, grinning at him over the table.

Adam glanced at her, but didn't smile and quickly looked away. Alex's heart dropped slightly. What was that about? They had had such a good day together, playing volleyball, walking by the lake, competing in the race. Had she done something wrong in there that she couldn't remember?

"I'd better go check on the sauce," Jenna's father said.

He was putting together a huge spaghetti dinner for all of them and had spent half the afternoon in the kitchen. All that separated the dining area from the kitchen was a long prepping counter, so Alex could see the big pot steaming away and could hear the sauce bubbling. According to Jenna, this whole cooking thing was pretty new for her recently divorced dad, so it took him an extra long time to make something basic. She had also requested that even if the food was totally gross, they all tell Mr. Bloom how much they loved it. "He needs positive feedback," Jenna had said.

"Why don't you kids set the table?" Mr. Bloom suggested.

"We're already on it!" Grace told him, walking out of the kitchen with a stack of plates.

"Hey, Adam?" Alex said hopefully. "Wanna help me fold the napkins?"

"Um, maybe when I'm done getting more chairs," Adam said quickly.

Then he turned around and practically ran out of the room. Alex felt Natalie watching her and looked down at the stack of napkins, pretending to concentrate on her folding. It was bad enough that Adam was acting so strangely toward her, but did he have to do it in front of all her friends?

Boys are weird, Alex reminded herself. *Just remember . . . boys . . . are . . . weird.*

For some reason it didn't make her feel any better.

A little while later, everyone was taking their seats at the table for dinner. Alex sat near the end, but made sure the seat next to hers was open. Brynn started to sit down in it, but Alex stopped her.

"I'm saving that one," Alex whispered.

Brynn paused and smiled. "I bet I know who for!" she sang. Alex blushed, but then Brynn quickly moved to a seat on the other side of the table.

Alex watched as Adam walked in with a basket

of bread and placed it on the table. He glanced around for a seat and his eyes fell on the one next to Alex. Her heart skipped a beat.

"See? Everything's fine," Natalie whispered to Alex, leaning in from her seat on Alex's right. "He's totally gonna come over here."

Alex smiled. Natalie was right. Everything was fine. She was just imagining things before.

But then Adam grabbed the chair that was directly in front of him and pulled it out. He sat down and grabbed a piece of bread without even looking in Alex's direction. Alex sunk down in her chair a bit and Natalie looked at her sympathetically.

"It's okay, Alex," Brynn whispered. "Maybe he just wanted to sit by his dad."

"Please. He couldn't have sat any farther away from me without sitting in the bathroom," Alex lamented. "Something's wrong."

Tori walked out of the bathroom after washing her hands and dropped down in the formerly "saved" seat. She looked around at the serious faces and her eyes widened.

"Uh-oh. What did I miss?" she asked.

"Adam didn't sit next to Alex," Brynn stated simply.

"Oh. Not good," Tori said, sucking some air through her teeth. This reaction did not make Alex feel better.

"What should I do, you guys?" she asked.

"Talk to him and find out what's up," Natalie suggested. "After dinner, of course."

"And say what?" Alex asked, the very idea making her stomach turn.

Natalie, Tori, and Brynn looked at one another blankly. "We're going to have to think about that one," Tori said.

Meanwhile, at the other end of the table, Jenna and David were going over their three-legged race, laughing about Jenna's near fall at the beginning and her real fall after the win.

"I totally saved you!" David said, taking a bite of his spaghetti. "If I hadn't caught your arm, you would have taken us both down."

"Would not!" Jenna said, blushing.

"I think I should start calling you Jenna the Klutz," David suggested.

Jenna whacked David's arm with the back of her hand and laughed. "You should *not!*" she cried.

Alex stared at Brynn across the table. "Is it just me or are those two flirting?" Brynn whispered.

"I was just thinking the same thing," Alex told her.

At the center of the table, Grace, Alyssa, and Valerie were engaged in a huge debate about *American Idol*, making enough noise that the other girls were able to talk without being heard.

"She just hit his arm," Tori pointed out. "That's a total crush signal."

She grabbed a roll and started to slap some butter onto it. Alex had no idea how she could do something that normal when there was a potential disaster happening before their eyes. Jenna was flirting with Sarah's boyfriend. Didn't Tori see how serious this was?

"Come on, you guys," Natalie said. "Jenna would never do that to Sarah."

"Well, she did have a crush on him once before," Alex pointed out. "Remember? Right before last year's social? Jenna totally wanted to go with David."

"I never knew that!" Tori said, her jaw dropping slightly.

"She's right. I remember," Natalie said, placing her bread back on her plate. "There was major drama."

"Yeah, but Jenna backed off," Brynn said. "Sarah told Jenna she liked David and that David liked her, and Jenna was cool about it."

At the other end of the table, Jenna said something funny and David nearly fell off his chair laughing. His eyes sparkled as he looked at Jenna. There was something about that look that made Alex suspicious. It was the way she *wished* Adam would look at *her* right now.

"Yeah, but the question is, does David *still* like Sarah?" Alex said. "Because he's sure acting like he likes Jenna."

"This could be trouble," Natalie said.

"Maybe Jenna shouldn't have signed up for the competition with him," Brynn whispered. "This morning she was all 'boys are gross,' but now . . ."

Jenna giggled and smiled at David over the top of her water glass as she took a sip.

"Now she's singing a different tune," Alex finished.

"We have to talk to her," Natalie said. "Just to make sure she's not crushing on him again. If she is, all three of them could get hurt. Jenna, David, *and* Sarah."

Alex sighed and took a sip of her own water. Now not only did *she* have to talk to *Adam*, but they *all* had to talk to Jenna? Who knew that a fun weekend away could turn into such a soap opera?

chapter SIX

Jenna smiled at her reflection in the bathroom mirror as she brushed her teeth. Today had been a very good day. She had won first place in the three-legged race with the added bonus of beating Adam. Grace had made some headway with her studying, and Jenna had gotten to dance with her friends. Plus there was all the delicious food and the sunshine and the rides they had gone on after dinner. All in all, it couldn't have been better.

"Hey, Jenna," Natalie said, appearing in the doorway in her tank top and pajama bottoms. "Can we talk to you for a sec?"

Jenna blinked. Who was "we," and what did they want to talk to her about? "Sure," she said through a mouth full of toothpaste. "I'll be right out."

Jenna rinsed her mouth out and wiped her face with a towel. When she walked back into the guest room, everyone was totally silent. Grace and Alyssa had already tucked their feet under the covers of one bed and Tori and Alex were sitting on the other. Brynn and Val sat on the floor on top of their sleeping bags with their backs propped up against one of the beds, and Natalie was just sort of hanging by the door.

"What's going on?" Jenna asked, feeling as if a spotlight was shining on her face.

Natalie looked at Alex, who nodded at her. This was really freaky. Never in her life had Jenna seen all of them so quiet all at the same time.

"We were just wondering what's up with you and David," Natalie said finally.

"Not that anything *is* up," Grace added quickly. "Personally, I don't think there is."

"But some of us kind of thought we maybe saw some . . . you know . . . sparks between the two of you at dinner tonight," Brynn said, her face screwed up apologetically.

Jenna's heart started to pound in her ears. The spotlight on her face grew hot. "You guys have to be kidding me," she said. "There were no sparks."

"That's what I thought!" Grace said with a breath of relief. "See? Now we can all just go to bed."

"Jenna, if you like him . . . it's okay, you know," Alyssa said, pulling her knees up under her chin.

"I don't like him!" Jenna replied. "He's *Sarah's* boyfriend."

"Exactly," Val said. "And Jenna would never, like, *go after* one of her friend's boyfriends."

"Yeah. Jenna's one of the most loyal friends on the planet," Grace put in.

"Thank you," Jenna said.

"I didn't say she was going after him," Alyssa said. "I just said she might like him. And if she does, it's okay. As long as she doesn't do anything to hurt Sarah, that's all."

Jenna felt angry tears prickling behind her eyes. How could her friends corner her like this and basically accuse her of trying to steal Sarah's boyfriend?

"Are you okay, Jenna?" Natalie asked, stepping forward. "I hope you're not mad. We were just worried about you, so we thought we should talk."

Suddenly Jenna realized that by standing there about to cry, she probably looked like she really *was* crushing on David again. And she so was not. She had gotten over that a million years ago. Besides, she would never start liking a friend's boyfriend. It just wasn't *her*.

So she pretended to laugh. "You guys are nuts," Jenna said, waving them off. "Just because David and I had fun competing today, that doesn't mean I have a crush on him. So you don't have to *worry* about me. I'm fine."

"You're sure," Alex said.

"Yes! I'm sure!" Jenna told them. She crossed over to the bed she was supposed to share with Tori that night and plopped down. "Now can we *please* talk about something else? I'm sick of boys already."

She saw Natalie and Brynn exchange an unconvinced glance and chose to ignore it.

"Hey! How's the routine coming?" Jenna asked Valerie, knowing that Val would jump at the chance to talk about the talent competition. It had become

Valerie's favorite subject of the weekend.

"It's great!" Valerie said, sitting up on her knees. "Brynn, Tori, Nat, and I finished it up this afternoon."

"Now all we have to do is teach it to everyone else," Tori said, checking her long blond ponytail for split ends.

"Wanna do it now?" Brynn asked, jumping up.

Jenna, Alex, and Grace all groaned. Jenna, for one, was exhausted from the day's excitement. And maybe she was crashing from a bit of a sugar high, too, what with all the cotton candy and ice cream she had eaten at the carnival.

"How about we do it first thing in the morning?" Alyssa suggested. "It's getting late, anyway."

"Sounds like a plan," Jenna said, crawling under the soft covers. "Nat? Could you get the light?"

"Got it!" Natalie said.

The room was doused in darkness and Jenna cuddled into her pillow, listening to the rest of her friends giggling and whispering as they settled into their sleeping bags. Tori lay flat on her back and closed her eyes, and Jenna rolled over on her side to face the wall. She closed her eyes and waited for her sleepiness to overtake her.

But two seconds later her eyes popped open again. Jenna stared at the striped wallpaper, her heart pounding. Because the second she had closed her eyes, all she had seen was David's face: the cute way he tossed his bangs off his forehead, the grin he'd given her before grabbing her into that hug. Somehow she suddenly couldn't stop thinking about him.

Were her friends right? Was she really crushing on David again?

▲ ▲ ▲

Something smacked Grace in the face and she woke up with a start. Her eyes crossed as she tried to figure out what was lying across her nose. Finally she recognized Alyssa's woven bracelet and giggled to herself. Apparently Alyssa was kind of a restless sleeper. Grace carefully lifted her friend's arm and placed it on the mattress next to her. Alyssa sighed in her sleep and rolled over. Grace would have to tell her about that one later.

The guest room was bathed in light and Grace glanced at the digital clock across the room. It was seven o'clock and everyone was still out cold. But in a couple of hours Valerie would be rousing them all for dance practice and another busy day would begin.

Grace yawned hugely. Part of her would have loved to have gone back to sleep, but she knew she had to study today and she didn't want to miss any of the fun. Maybe if she got up and got the work over with now, she wouldn't have to miss out. It sounded like a solid plan to her. So with some effort, she forced herself to get up out of bed and grab her textbook from the top of the dresser. She gathered up the flash cards Alyssa had helped her make the day before. Then she tiptoed across the room, stepping over Val's outstretched hand and Brynn's mop of hair, and opened the door as quietly as possible. She slipped out and closed it behind her, then let out a breath.

"I'm so good," she whispered to herself. "I should be a spy."

Downstairs, Grace poured herself a glass of orange juice and took it to the dining room table where her book and flash cards were already laid out. She sat down and pulled the first card to her. Suddenly she felt very proud of herself for being so responsible. Her mother was always telling her that if she made time for her work she would enjoy her fun time that much more, but Grace had never really listened. Imagine how surprised her mother would be if she could see Grace now!

Grace read the block lettering on the front of the first card. "Lincoln elected president," she whispered. She squeezed her eyes closed and concentrated. "1850!"

She turned the card over and her heart sank. "1860," she read aloud. With a deep breath, she set it aside. "Okay, that was just the first one," she told herself. "Just getting warmed up."

The next card stared up at her. The block letters read: FIRST BATTLE OF BULL RUN. Grace stared back at the card. Her mind was a complete and total blank. Suddenly, she started to panic. She had known this yesterday. She was *sure* that she had. So why could she not remember it at all today?

"Okay, think about this logically," she told herself. "You know the Civil War got started after President Lincoln was elected, so if he was elected in 1850 . . ."

She glanced at the last card and winced. "I mean, 1860 . . ."

Grace covered her face with her hands. What was wrong with her? She couldn't even remember one fact for five seconds? Suddenly her body let out a huge yawn and she sighed.

Maybe she was just too tired. Maybe studying this early in the morning wasn't a good idea. But she had to. She had to try to concentrate if she wanted to hang out with her friends later. The last thing she wanted was to have this book hanging over her head all day. But her head felt *so* heavy.

Grace took a deep breath and rested her chin on her arms. She stared at the card.

The Battle of Bull Run . . . The Battle of Bull Run . . . she repeated in her head. Pretty soon, her eyes were drooping. Then hundreds of bulls were running through her mind, stampeding over thousands and thousands of flash cards. And before Grace knew it, she had fallen completely asleep.

▲ ▲ ▲

"I'm voting for pancakes!" someone shouted at the top of their lungs.

Grace's head popped up and she blinked a couple dozen times. Nothing around her was familiar. Where was she? Why was there a piece of paper stuck to her face? She yanked it away and saw one of the flash cards with the smudged word ANTIETAM on the front. Everything came back to her in a rush. She was at Jenna's lake house, at the dining table outside the kitchen. She had gotten up early to study and . . .

She couldn't believe it. She had fallen asleep in

the middle of studying! Grace checked her pink plastic watch and her eyes widened. Apparently she had been asleep here for an hour. How embarrassing! She hoped no one had seen her!

With a disappointed sigh, Grace looked around at her books and notes. Instantly, she felt overwhelmed. She had absorbed exactly nothing and now, from the sounds of it, everyone else was already up.

Why am I so bad at this? Grace wondered, her shoulders slumping. *Why can't I just concentrate and learn something?*

Seconds later, Jenna, Natalie, and Val all bounded into the room, showered, dressed, and full of life.

"Pancakes with butter and syrup and . . ."

Jenna stopped short when she saw Grace sitting all bleary-eyed at the end of the table. Natalie and Val almost barreled right into Jenna's back. Valerie was already wearing her workout clothes for their dance rehearsal. A rehearsal it looked like Grace was going to have to miss—again. Grace could hear all the other girls on the stairs, chatting and laughing as they made their way down.

"There you are!" Val said. "We were wondering what had happened to you!"

Natalie stepped forward, her expression concerned. She must have noticed how miserable Grace looked.

"Are you okay?" she asked.

"No. No, I'm not," Grace said, slapping her book closed. "It's Sunday already and I've learned exactly nothing! There's no way I'm ever going to pass this test, and then I'm going to have to go to summer school and miss camp!"

Grace was on the verge of tears. Frustrated, tired tears.

"It can't be that bad," Jenna said. "You studied for two whole hours yesterday and you knew it then."

"I know! But now I don't remember anything," Grace said, pushing away from the table. "I missed out on dancing and all that for nothing."

The other girls had joined them now and they were all looking at Grace with wide eyes as if she might explode. Well, she kind of felt like exploding. That's how frustrated she was. But with everyone staring at her, she just felt like a big old baby. A big old baby who was spoiling everyone's good time.

"Sorry. Forget it," she said. "I'll be upstairs."

Then she turned on her heel and made a break for it, taking the steps two at a time. By the time she got to the bathroom off the guest room, she was working really hard to keep from bursting into tears. She ran inside and closed the door behind her, dropping down on the toilet seat.

What was she going to do? If she didn't find a way to pass this test, she wouldn't be seeing her friends again for a whole year. They would all go off to camp without her and she would have to spend the whole summer studying and feeling left out. Sometimes being a seventh-grader could be really unfair.

chapter
SEVEN

Grace stood up and ran some cold water into the sink. She splashed her face with it and stared into her own eyes in the mirror. That felt a little better. Now if only she could erase the last five minutes from her friends' memories.

There was a light knock on the bathroom door.

"Grace? It's Alyssa."

"And Val," Valerie added quietly.

Grace grabbed a towel and held it to her face. She felt so silly for storming out. She didn't want to talk to anyone. "I kind of want to be alone right now," she said, her voice muffled by the towel.

"Please open the door," Alyssa begged. "We just want to make sure you're okay."

Grace took a deep breath. She stared at the happy flowers on the shower curtain for a moment before turning and cracking the door open. With one eye, she peeked out.

"Hey," Alyssa said sympathetically.

"Hi," Grace replied, biting her lip. "Sorry about that."

"It's okay. You're stressed out," Valerie said with a shrug. "It happens to everyone."

One look at Valerie's stretchy shorts and tank top and Grace's heart sank. She didn't know a single step of Valerie's dance routine, and it looked as if she wouldn't be learning them. Not this morning, anyway.

"I think I ruined your whole morning-rehearsal idea," Grace said, opening the door the rest of the way. "I'm sorry."

"Please!" Val said, walking into the small bathroom. She leaned back against the wall and crossed her arms over her stomach. "Your test is a lot more important. Who cares about some random talent competition?"

"You do!" Grace pointed out. "You're so excited about it, and so are Brynn and Tori and Nat. But there's no way I'm going to have time to learn a whole dance. I feel like I'm letting everyone down."

"First of all, you're not letting anyone down," Alyssa told her, slinging her arm around Grace's neck. "It's not like everyone's downstairs right now crying into their pancakes. They're all trying to figure out ways to help you."

"They are?" Grace asked.

"We want you to come to camp," Alyssa told her. "That matters more than anything else."

"It wouldn't be the same without you," Valerie agreed.

Grace felt warm from the top of her head all the way down to her toes. She smiled. "Thanks, guys."

"Besides, this weekend is supposed to be fun,"

Valerie said. "And we always have fun as long as we're hanging out together, right? Whether we're dancing or studying."

"That is true," Grace said. She was so glad she had such amazing friends. A few minutes ago she had been miserable, but already she was feeling much better.

"Wait a minute! Val! You just gave me an idea!" Alyssa said, her eyes brightening.

Val looked at her, confused. "I did? How?"

"Dancing *and* studying!" Alyssa said, clasping her hands together. "Why didn't I think of this before?"

Grace and Valerie stared at each other. "Do you have any idea what she's talking about?" Grace joked.

"Not a clue," Valerie replied. "She may have finally lost it."

Alyssa ignored them. She was clearly too excited to care about their teasing. "I think I know of a way that we can help Grace with her studying and still pull off the talent show," she said.

Now Grace was downright interested. She pushed herself away from the sink just as Valerie stepped away from the wall. They faced Alyssa together.

"Tell us more," Valerie said.

▲ ▲ ▲

It was a beautiful, summery day and the sun was high in the sky as Jenna walked over to the starting line for the wheelbarrow race. All morning she and her friends had helped Alyssa, Grace, and Val work on Alyssa's new studying plan, and it had been a lot of fun. They had already decided to work on it some more later that afternoon, but for now, Jenna was ready to focus on racing—and hopefully winning.

Excitement skittered through her veins when she saw all the competitors getting ready to go. There was nothing Jenna loved more than a good race. She just wished her friends hadn't spent so much time talking about David the night before. Because now, no matter what she did, she couldn't stop thinking about him.

Which was *really* annoying her.

What would Sarah think if she knew that Jenna had been stealing glances at David all through breakfast? What would she think if she knew that right now Jenna's heart was beating extra fast as she wondered where David was? *Did* she really have a crush on David? Again?

I am the worst friend ever, Jenna thought as she lifted her foot behind her and grabbed it to stretch her quad muscle.

But then she remembered what Alyssa had said. If she did have a crush on David, which she wasn't willing to admit yet, there was nothing wrong with that. A person couldn't control their feelings. What she could control were her actions. As long as she didn't do anything about her crush, she was okay. In fact, ignoring her feelings made her an even *better* friend. Because she was doing it for Sarah.

Besides, it wasn't like David was crushing on *her*. Then she would be in real trouble.

"Hey, partner."

Jenna's heart jumped and skipped about ten beats. Somehow David had snuck up behind her.

Okay, it's just David. Just one of Adam's dork friends. Just think of him that way. It's no big deal, she told herself.

She turned around slowly. David grinned down at her. He was wearing a white track T-shirt from his middle school and his arms and face were all tan from spending yesterday in the sun.

I do not think he's cute. I do not think he's cute, Jenna said to herself over and over.

"Hey," she said casually, even though she knew her face was turning red. Hopefully he'd think it was just a sunburn.

"You ready to win this thing?" he asked, slapping her on the back.

Jenna's heart thumped again. "Totally," she said.

Down by the starting line, Alex and Adam stood a few feet away from each other looking awkward. Every time Adam looked at Alex, Alex looked away. They both stretched their arms over their head and tried not to notice each other. What was going on with those two? One second they were all buddy-buddy and ooey-gooey, and the next it was like they were sworn enemies. Jenna could not imagine ever being part of a couple. It just seemed too complicated.

The same announcer from the day before grabbed a microphone near the finish line. Today, for some reason, he was wearing a big black top hat with a red flower on it.

"Okay, competitors!" he said into the mic. "Everyone get ready! We're about to start."

"How about I hold your ankles first?" David asked.

Jenna nodded. There was a lump of nervousness in her throat and another in her stomach. "Sure."

She stepped in front of David and crouched on the ground, putting her hands in the grass and her feet behind her. Glancing to her left she saw that Adam was doing the same. Alex stood behind him, looking almost grim. Jenna wondered if her friend's pulse was racing as fast as Jenna's was. It sure didn't seem like it. Alex didn't look excited at all. About the race *or* about Adam.

"Okay, on your marks! Get set!" the announcer shouted.

Please, please, please let us win! Jenna thought.

"Go!"

The starter pistol went off and David grabbed Jenna's ankles. Her stomach swooped as her legs were lifted into the air and instantly she started to run—with her hands. Never in her life had she felt so strong and coordinated. Her hands shot out one after the other and soon they were far ahead of the couple next to them, gunning for the switch line. Once they got there, Jenna would have to get up and hold David's ankles.

"Go, Jenna!" her friends shouted from the sideline. "You can do it!"

"Switch!" David shouted. The moment Jenna's hands crossed the white line, David dropped her ankles. Hard. Her toes hit the ground with a slam.

"Ow!" Jenna shouted.

"Oops! Sorry," David said.

He dropped on the ground and shoved out his long legs. Jenna limped around to grab them, but when she tried to hoist them, the right leg slipped out of her grasp. A few pairs zoomed by them, including Alex and Adam.

"Ouch! Hey! Was that payback?" David joked, glancing over his shoulder.

Jenna rolled her eyes and picked up his legs, using all her strength. "Okay. Go! Go! Go!" she shouted at him.

David jolted forward and started to "run." Jenna struggled to keep control of his crazy-long and heavy legs. They passed one couple, then another. A third completely lost it and fell into the dirt. On the sidelines, Jenna could hear her friends screaming themselves hoarse.

"Go, Jenna! Go, Alex!"

Right before the finish line, David picked up the pace and shot ahead of another couple. Everyone in the crowd cheered and shouted and jumped around. David crossed over the line and collapsed his elbows, tumbling over into the grass. His chest heaved up and down. Surprised, Jenna tripped over him, but righted herself before she could crash into the ground. She had no idea if they had placed in the race. She was just glad they had finished at all.

"Congratulations to our winners!" the announcer called out, handing a pair of blue ribbons to Adam and Alex.

The two of them jumped up and down and hugged, smiling like crazy. Whatever ice wall had gone up between them, winning the race had smashed it down. Jenna and Alex's friends rushed over to Alex to congratulate her on her win. Jenna was green with envy. Adam and Alex had beaten her and David!

"And to our second-place winners!" the announcer said, making his way over to Jenna. He handed her two red ribbons.

"We came in second?" she asked, shocked.

"Don't be so surprised!" the announcer said. "That was a fine race!"

Jenna looked down at David and laughed as the man moved away. "Second place!" she cheered, throwing both her hands up with the ribbons. "We can still win the whole thing if we do well in the balloon toss tomorrow."

David lifted his head from the ground. "That's great," he said, lifting a hand toward her. "Think you can help me up now?"

Jenna snorted, but grabbed his arm. She yanked him up so hard he almost fell into her. Jenna ignored the embarrassed blush that came over her. She was too psyched to worry about it. She handed David one of the red ribbons and he looked down at it with pride.

"We make a good team," he said.

Jenna grinned. "Sure do."

David looked at her and something in his eyes changed. They softened somehow. "You're really cool, Jenna," he said.

Jenna's still-pounding heart slowed. Suddenly she had butterflies dancing like crazy all through her stomach. She felt very, very warm.

"Uh . . . thanks," she said.

"You're, like, *really* cool," David said.

He was staring at her with this very serious

expression. The kind of expression the guys on those teen soaps always had on before they kissed someone.

Oh, no. He doesn't want to kiss me, does he? Jenna thought, panicking.

Then, over his shoulder, Jenna saw her friends jogging toward her to congratulate her. They could not catch her and David right now. She didn't know why she felt that, but she just did.

"I gotta go!" she blurted.

Then, before she could even think about how quickly his face had fallen, she ran right around him and into Brynn's waiting arms.

"Second place! Congrats!" Brynn shouted.

"Yeah! Nice work!" Grace cheered, patting Jenna on the back.

"Thanks, guys," Jenna said.

"Not as good as first, though," Alex teased, holding up her ribbon.

"Ha-ha," Jenna said. "Just wait until tomorrow! You guys are going down!"

"Come on. Let's get something to eat before these two *really* start trash talking," Tori said, slinging her arm over Natalie's shoulder.

"Food! Food good!" Jenna said with a caveman growl, rubbing her red ribbon on her stomach.

Everyone laughed and Jenna walked off with all her friends around her. She glanced back once to see David chatting with Adam like nothing had happened. And maybe nothing had. Maybe she had imagined the whole thing.

A girl could hope.

chapter

EIGHT

"Okay, everyone! Line up!" Valerie called out.

Grace scrambled into place between Alex and Jenna. The sun shone down on her face and a few fluffy clouds chased one another across the sky. Down at the lake, kids shouted and splashed and chased each other along the water's edge, the still frigid lake licking at their toes. Unlike this morning, Grace was now loving every minute of this vacation. Alyssa's plan was genius.

"Ready?" Tori asked.

"Ready!" everyone chorused.

Tori hit the play button on the CD player and jumped into position near the front of the group. Grace smiled as the music started up.

"Five, six, seven, eight!" Val called out.

Grace and her friends launched into the dance. A twirl here, some funky footwork there. But they weren't just dancing. They were also singing.

"The Confederate Constitution signed in

1861! Just a few days after Lincoln was sworn in!" they sang. "In April of that very same year, the South took Fort Sumter, which the president held dear!"

Grace caught Alyssa's eye as they slid past each other, switching formation, and they both grinned. Alyssa, Grace, and Val had spent half the morning changing all the words to the song to include facts about the Civil War. Now, suddenly, Grace could remember everything. Straight memorization hadn't stuck, but this was really working. Alyssa had made a bunch of boring dates and names into a fun song. And now, *all* the girls knew all the words.

Plus it meant that Grace could go over everything over and over and over again, while learning Val's dance at the same time. Alyssa really *had* found a way for both Grace and Val to be happy.

"The South held the fort till 1865," Grace sang with her friends, clapping and then waving her arms in the air. "The brave soldiers of the South there kept the Confederates' hopes alive!"

Grace laughed and jumped into her next move. This had to be the best studying session she'd ever had in her life. And it was a lot more fun than ever before, too.

Alex linked arms with Brynn as she and her friends tromped across the picnic grounds toward the gazebo that night. Everyone was in high spirits, singing the words to their Civil War song, skipping and twirling one another around. Up ahead, the large white gazebo was strung with colorful paper lanterns that bobbed in the light breeze. Alex could hear a slow, romantic song being played by the five-piece band on the raised stage. All around the gazebo people milled about, all dressed up for the dance. The women wore sundresses and some had flowers in their hair. The men had mostly worn slacks and short-sleeved shirts, but some had on jackets and there were even a few ties. A man in a striped jacket sold lemonade and a couple of little kids ran by, chasing one another with sparklers.

"This is amazing, Jenna," Tori said. "I feel like I just stepped onto a movie set."

"But it's all real," Brynn put in. "Freakishly, time-warpily real."

"Time-warpily?" Alyssa said, raising an eyebrow.

"It's vacation. I can make up words," Brynn joked.

Alex felt the denim skirt she had borrowed from Natalie start to ride up and she yanked down on the hem. Everyone had decided to wear their most stylish outfits for the dance, but Alex hadn't brought along anything appropriate. No one had told her there was going to be a dance. Luckily, Natalie always overpacked and always had nothing but the latest fashions on hand. Unluckily, Alex had never been fully comfortable in skirts and tank tops.

"You okay?" Brynn asked as Alex fiddled with the strap on her tank.

"Yeah," Alex said, making herself smile. "Just adjusting to high fashion."

"Well, it looks amazing on you, if that helps,"

Natalie said. "Adam is going to drool when he sees you."

Alex brightened a bit. "You think?"

"Are you kidding? The kid would have to be sleeping not to," Tori said.

"Or blind," Val put in.

"Or just really really stupid," Alyssa joked.

"That's the one!" Jenna announced. "That's my brother! Really *really* stupid."

Everyone laughed. Everyone but Alex. She knew that teasing Adam was one of Jenna's favorite pastimes, but it was weird for her now. She really liked Adam, so it was hard to listen to someone mocking him. At least she knew that Jenna didn't always mean it. Jenna loved her brother, she just didn't like her friends to know it.

"Oh, it's so pretty," Alyssa said as they arrived near the steps to the gazebo. On the wood floor, dozens of couples swirled and swayed to the music. "I love all the lanterns. And look! These are real roses!"

She reached up to finger the petals on one of the vines that had been wound around the gazebo's pillars. That was Alyssa. Always appreciating the beauty around her. All Alex could do was look around at the crowd and wonder if Adam was there anywhere. She didn't see him.

"Do you think the guys are really coming to this?" she asked, trying to sound casual.

"Are you kidding? Boys avoid dances like I avoid vegetables," Jenna said.

"Uh, Jenna. Might want to take that one back," Val said, pointing. "Check it out."

Sure enough, Adam, David, and Mr. Bloom were slowly making their way around the gazebo. They each had a cup of lemonade, and were laughing and chatting as they walked. Adam was wearing a striped button-down short-sleeved shirt unlike anything Alex had ever seen him wear. His normally messy brown hair was combed neatly and he looked . . . adorable.

"Wow. Those boys clean up well," Tori said, impressed.

David had worn a nice sweater over shorts, and Jenna's dad had on a tie and jacket.

"Good evening, everyone!" Mr. Bloom said as the guys joined them. "Don't we all look nice tonight?"

"Oh, Mr. Bloom. These old getups?" Brynn joked, looking down at her brand-new blue sundress.

Alex looked hopefully at Adam, waiting for the reaction that all the girls had said he would have. He glanced at her, blushed, and quickly looked away. No drool whatsoever. Not that she had *actually* been expecting drool. But a smile or a compliment might have been nice.

Ask me to dance, Alex willed him. *Look how romantic it all is!*

Adam cleared his throat and looked at her again. Alex's heart skipped a beat. *Here it comes!*

"You okay, son?" his father said, slapping him on the back. "Not getting a cold, I hope."

Adam reddened even further. "Uh, no. I'm fine," he said. And suddenly he was staring at his feet. Where was Alex's invitation to dance?

"So . . . Jenna," David said out of nowhere.

"Wanna dance?"

Alex gaped at David. For that matter, so did all the other girls. The eight of them, who had been twittering and whispering and giggling moments ago, were now completely silent. Jenna's face went white.

"What?" she said.

"It's a dance, right?" David said, gesturing at the gazebo. "So do you want to?"

Jenna looked like she was about to be sick. "Uh, no thanks," she said quickly.

David's face fell and Mr. Bloom stepped in. "Jenna. If a nice young gentleman asks you for a dance, it's rude to turn him down," he said. "Besides, you should all be having fun. So get out there!"

Jenna stared at her father as if he had just turned her over to the enemy in the middle of Capture the Flag. Finally she just ducked her head and muttered, "Fine."

"Great!" David said brightly. He handed his half-empty cup of lemonade to Adam and grabbed Jenna's hand. "Let's go," he said, hauling her off.

"This could be trouble," Brynn sang quietly.

Mr. Bloom was totally clueless that anything odd was going on. "Well, I'm going to go get some ice cream," he said. "Any of you girls want anything?"

"No. No thanks!" the girls chorused.

Alex stared at Adam, wondering if she'd somehow become invisible. He looked at her one last time, but she had no idea what he was thinking.

"I'll come with you, Dad," he said.

The two of them turned and walked off together,

weaving their way through the crowd. Adam dumped both his lemonade and David's in the trash and never looked back.

"Sorry, Alex," Grace said the moment they were gone. "I really thought he was going to ask you to dance."

"I don't get it," Alex said. She got a sudden chill and wrapped her hands around her bare arms. "Isn't he happy to see me?"

"Of course he is!" Brynn said. "He asked you to play volleyball yesterday, right?"

"And you guys have looked totally chummy at all the olde-tyme events," Tori pointed out.

"Yeah, but every other time I see him, he totally ignores me," Alex said. "It's like I'm not even there, and I'm supposed to be his girlfriend!"

"I don't get it," Val said. "I mean, you either like a person or you don't like a person. And if you *like* a person you should be nice to them all the time."

Alex's heart squeezed in her chest. Valerie had just said exactly what Alex had been thinking all weekend long.

"Maybe he only likes me because I'm a good athlete," Alex said. "Like I'm a good person to join races with and do sports with, but not to be boyfriend-and-girlfriend with. Maybe I'm just one of the guys to him."

Natalie slipped her arm over Alex's shoulders. "I'm sure that's not it. I mean, how could anyone look at a girl as pretty as you and think 'just one of the guys'?"

"Seriously, Alex," Alyssa said. "Adam is just new

to this whole boyfriend-girlfriend thing. Like you are. He's just figuring it all out."

"I hope so," Alex said with a sigh.

Unfortunately, she couldn't stop thinking about what Valerie had said. It should be that simple. If you like someone, you're nice to them. If you don't like someone, you're not nice to them. All these mixed signals Adam was giving her were going to drive her nuts.

Suddenly Alex realized that everyone was looking at her with hopeful pity and it made her want to squirm. She hated being the center of attention unless it was out on the soccer field. So she decided to change the subject.

"Know what *I* can't figure out? Jenna and David," Alex said, looking past Tori at the gazebo.

Everyone turned around and Alex felt relieved to be out from under their stares. Instead, they were all looking at Jenna now. Her arms were around David's neck and his arms were around her waist. They stepped from side to side in the center of the gazebo. David was looking down at Jenna, but Jenna was pointedly gazing off over his shoulder.

"I can't believe he asked Jenna to dance," Val said. "What about Sarah?"

"I'm starting to think that David doesn't like Sarah anymore," Alyssa said. "I think he likes Jenna now."

"You're right," Natalie said. "Look at the way he's looking at her!"

"He's a goner," Tori said with a nod. "Poor Sarah."

"Do you think we should call Sarah and tell her

what's going on?" Alex asked.

"And tattle on Jenna? No way!" Grace said.

"But it wouldn't be tattling on Jenna because Jenna hasn't done anything wrong," Val said.

"Unless she does like him back," Natalie pointed out.

"Do you really think she does?" Brynn asked.

They all stared at Jenna. She looked pretty miserable, but that didn't mean much. Even if she liked the guy, she would probably feel awkward dancing with him since he *was* going out with one of her friends.

"It doesn't even matter," Val said. "Sarah deserves to know that her boyfriend is asking other girls to dance."

"I don't know, you guys," Tori said, hugging herself as a cool breeze kicked up. "What's Sarah going to do about it from home?"

"We should let David handle it," Alyssa said diplomatically. "If he likes Jenna then he should break up with Sarah."

"Yeah. She should hear it from David, not from us," Brynn agreed.

"But what if he *doesn't* tell Sarah?" Alex said, her stomach squirming. "We've already decided that boys are weird. Just because we would do the right thing, that doesn't mean he would."

This made all the girls fall silent again. They turned and looked at Jenna and David dancing under the lights. David really did have stars in his eyes. Meanwhile, Sarah was sitting at home thinking her boyfriend still totally liked her. Alex was starting to think that boys weren't just weird, they were also mean. Between Adam and David, it was clear that boys never thought about anyone's feelings other than their own.

▲ ▲ ▲

Jenna could tell her friends were whispering about her. Every time she looked over there they were staring at her and David, and they kept ducking their heads together to talk. She just wished this stupid song would end already. Her stomach was in nervous knots, and she felt awkward and warm with her arms around David's neck. So warm that she was pretty sure her wrists were starting to sweat and they were going to leave stains on his sweater. Who knew wrists could sweat?

"Think we're gonna win the balloon toss tomorrow?" David asked.

"Depends," Jenna replied, trying to sound normal. "Are you any good?"

"I can throw a water balloon with the best of them," David replied with a grin.

Jenna started to smile, but then bit her tongue. Instead, she lifted her shoulders. "Then we have a chance," she said.

David pulled back a little and looked down at her. "Are you mad at me or something?" he asked.

With a deep breath, Jenna managed to look him in the eye. Big mistake. He had the nicest eyes *ever*. She quickly looked away.

"Why would I be mad at you?" she asked.

Maybe because you might want to kiss me and cheat on

one of my best friends? she thought. *And even worse, I might want you to kiss me? If I even knew what kissing felt like . . .*

"I don't know," David said. "That's kinda why I'm asking."

Jenna sighed and the song finally plucked its way to a close. Everyone stopped dancing and applauded for the band. Everyone except Jenna. All she wanted to do was get out of there as fast as possible.

"Well, thanks," she said, pulling her arms away and backing up. "That was fun."

Or torture, depending on how you look at it.

"Jenna, wait," David said.

Jenna's breath caught in her throat. She knew she should just turn around and walk away, but for some reason she couldn't move. David took a step closer to her.

"I just wanted to tell you something," he said.

"What?" she asked. Her heart was pounding a million times a minute.

"I wanted to tell you that . . . I like you," David said. "I mean I *really* like you."

Jenna couldn't have swallowed or breathed if her life depended on it. In that moment she knew that she had been hoping he would say that. She really *was* a bad friend.

"But . . . but you're with Sarah," she said.

"I know I am," David said. "And I like Sarah, too, but not the same way anymore. Not like I like you."

Jenna felt as if she was going to melt right there, but she made herself think of her friend. This was Sarah's boyfriend. *Sarah's* boyfriend. And as much as she liked him back, it didn't matter. As long as he was Sarah's boyfriend, she couldn't tell him how she felt. And he shouldn't have been telling her either.

"I have to go," she said.

Then she did manage to turn and run out of there—fast. She sprinted right through the crowd of dancers, down the steps, and past her friends. She even stepped on a few feet as she went, but she didn't stop to see whose feet they were. She just threw a few "sorrys" over her shoulder and hoped that everyone would recover.

"Jenna! Jenna, wait! Where're you going?" Brynn shouted.

But Jenna didn't stop. She had to get away from David. That was the only thing she could think about right then.

chapter

NINE

"I love fireworks!" Brynn said excitedly as she helped Jenna spread out the two blankets they had taken from the linen closet. One was covered in pink flowers and the other was red and blue plaid. "There should be fireworks every weekend of the year instead of just special occasions."

The grass underneath the blankets made them all bumpy, so Grace crouched down to smooth them out. "I second that!" she said.

"But if they had them every weekend, they wouldn't be special," Alyssa said as she dropped down on her knees. Then she looked up at her friends, wide-eyed. "Oh, man. I just sounded exactly like my mother!"

Everyone laughed and Alex forced herself to smile. Her friends seemed to be having so much more fun than she was. All over the park, families and couples set up beach chairs or sat down on towels to await the big fireworks display. Kids wore glow necklaces and bracelets and ran around, waving their arms to make streaks of light in the dark. A few older teenagers walked through the crowd selling ice cream and cotton candy. There was a buzz of excitement in the air, but Alex just felt annoyed. All she could think about anymore was Adam. Where was he? What was he doing? Was he thinking about her? Did he still want to be her boyfriend or not? She was sick of it. She wanted to be having fun like her friends. This whole boyfriend thing was just not worth it.

Alex knew what she had to do to save her weekend. Maybe even her entire summer at Camp Lakeview. It wasn't going to be easy, but it had to be done. She narrowed her eyes and scanned the crowd. It was already dark out and Alex knew it wouldn't be easy to find Adam in this mess. Of course, there was one good place to start. Like Jenna, Adam liked his food, so Alex glanced from popcorn vendor to ice cream truck to hot dog cart, checking all the lines.

"Alex? What're you doing?" Jenna asked, looking up at her. "You look like an angry statue or something."

"Yeah! Come sit!" Natalie said, whipping out a pack of cards. "We're going to have a spit tournament until the fireworks start."

"Count me out," Grace said. She pulled out her textbook and a flashlight. "I have a little more studying to do."

"What about you, Alex?" Brynn asked. She yanked out a bottle of bug-repelling baby oil and started spreading it on her arms. "Are you in?"

Suddenly Alex spotted Adam and David. Sure enough, they were hovering near the hot dog stand at the far end of the field. The instant Alex saw Adam, she rolled her shoulders back and screwed up her courage.

"I'll play winners in the second round," she told her friends. "I'll be right back."

She saw a few of the girls exchange curious glances as she walked away, but she ignored them. Right now, Alex had a one-track mind. Her heart pounded painfully as she stalked across the grass, making sure not to step on anyone's hands or feet, but she ignored her heart, too. If she was going to start acting normal again and stop obsessing about Adam, she had to do this now.

"Adam!" she shouted from a few feet away.

He and David both looked up and smiled. Of course. An hour ago he couldn't even look her in the eye, but now he was smiling at her. One look at that cute grin and part of her wanted to forget the whole thing, but she knew that his friendly attitude was only temporary. Tomorrow he'd be all mean to her again and she would be miserable. It was time to get this over with.

"Hey, Alex!" Adam shouted back. "We have a sheet set up over by the path. Want to come hang out with us?"

"No," Alex said, making her way toward him. "No, I don't."

Adam's face fell. "What's wrong?"

By now Alex was standing only a foot away from him. "Look, Adam, I don't know what your problem is this weekend, but I am so sick of the way you're acting," Alex ranted, her face heating up.

"Uh, I'll be over here," David said, turning and

walking away to give his friends some privacy.

"What do you mean?" Adam asked, stunned.

"I mean . . . well . . . you either like a person or you don't like a person," Alex said, repeating Val's words from earlier that night. The words that had sounded so wise.

"What?" Adam said.

"And if you like a person then you're nice to them *all* the time," Alex continued. "Not just when you feel like it."

"Alex—"

"I thought you liked me, but I guess I was wrong," Alex said, crossing her arms. "So I don't think we should be boyfriend and girlfriend anymore, okay?"

Adam stared at Alex like she had just turned into a vampire right in front of him. "O . . . okay," he said finally.

Alex felt as if someone had just shot her through the chest with an arrow. Adam wasn't even going to tell her she was wrong? He wasn't even going to try to fight her decision?

It looked as if he really *didn't* like her anymore.

"Fine," she said.

Then she turned around, her dark hair flying, and stormed off. Tears sprung from the corners of her eyes and she quickly wiped them away with the backs of her hands. She couldn't believe it. She and Adam had just broken up. Alex Kim had just broken up with the first boy she had ever liked. If there was one thing she had never thought this weekend would bring, it was a breakup.

With a deep breath, Alex lifted her head and tried to look as if nothing was wrong. She just hoped that by the time she got back to her friends' blankets, they wouldn't be able to tell that she had been crying. Because she was done talking about Adam Bloom. Done talking about him, done thinking about him, just done.

As of this moment, Alex was over boys.

"Yes! I win! I sooooo dominate!" Jenna cried, thrusting her fists in the air. She had just beaten Brynn in the first round of their spit tournament. "I am the spit master!"

"I don't think that's something you want to be shouting at the top of your lungs," Brynn said grumpily, swinging her legs around so that she could lie down and look up at the sky. "At least not in a public place."

Jenna dropped her arms and looked around. Several people *were* looking at her in a disturbed way. "So what?" she said, shaking her curls behind her shoulders. "I did beat you."

"And you wouldn't be Jenna Bloom if you didn't rub it in," Grace said. She looked up from her book long enough to reach over and pat Jenna on the back.

Jenna grinned. "Exactly."

At that moment, Alex returned to the blanket and dropped down, hard. She had a look of extreme concentration on her face. Like she was trying to do algebra in her head. Something about it made Jenna's senses go on alert. She glanced at Brynn and saw that Brynn looked concerned as well.

"Alex? Everything okay?" Brynn asked.

"Oh, yeah. Everything's fine," Alex said, shrugging. "I just broke up with Adam."

Jenna's heart dropped. "What?" she asked.

"Alex! When? How?" Natalie asked.

Suddenly everyone was gathered around Alex. She didn't look all that comfortable with everyone watching her, but still. You did not make an announcement like that and expect everyone to just shrug. The girl had to explain.

"I just decided to do it," Alex said. "Just now. I was thinking about what we talked about before and Valerie was right. If Adam really liked me, he would be nice to me. And he hasn't been very nice to me this weekend."

"But that's just my brother. He's a doof," Jenna said.

"I thought you'd be happy about this," Alex said to Jenna. "You always thought it was weird that your brother was going out with one of us."

Jenna squirmed. "Yeah, it was weird. But it's not like I want to see you unhappy. Either one of you."

"I'll be fine," Alex told them. "Let's just . . . let's just talk about something else."

Everyone looked around the circle at everyone else, clearly confused and sad for Alex. It seemed as if no one could come up with a good subject change. What did you say to a girl when she'd just broken up with her first boyfriend ever? This was new territory for Jenna. Natalie had broken up with Simon, but she'd done it in the middle of the winter, so most of her communication had been via e-mail. The girls had never been together for an in-person breakup.

One thing Jenna knew for sure was that she couldn't say anything about the bright side of the situation. It was only a bright side for *her*. If Alex and Adam had broken up, then Adam and David probably wouldn't be crashing her little fireworks party. Which meant she wouldn't have to deal with being around David for the next couple of hours. She had no idea what to say to him now that he'd told her he liked her. Zero idea. Zilch.

But thanks to Alex, Jenna was safe. For now.

"So . . . Jenna," Natalie said. "What's the deal with you and David? For real this time."

Jenna turned beet red. Okay, so maybe she *wasn't* safe.

"This again?" she said, rolling her eyes.

Jenna hadn't told her friends that David had said he liked her. Normally she would have gone straight to the girls and told them everything, then asked for their advice. But this wasn't a normal situation. One of their friend's boyfriends had told *another* friend that he liked *her* instead. Who knew whose side everyone would take? All Jenna knew for sure was that the whole thing would be dramatic and messy. Plus no one would be able to stop talking about it. And that was the last thing she wanted to do for the rest of the weekend.

For the millionth time she wished that her father had let her and her friends come alone. No Adam would mean no David. Which would mean that none of this would have happened.

"You guys looked pretty cozy out there on the dance floor," Tori said.

"So? You've gotta touch the guy when you dance," Jenna said. "Otherwise it's not dancing."

She dropped back onto her elbows and looked up at the darkening sky, willing the fireworks to start already. They couldn't exactly talk about boys over the sound of ten million explosions.

"Yeah, but the point is, you *did* dance with him," Natalie said. "Normally you don't want to go anywhere near boys."

"Ew! Boy cooties!" Brynn teased.

"I only danced with him because my father made me!" Jenna said, sitting up straight again. "You guys saw it! You were right there!"

"All we're saying is, it seems like you guys are having a lot of fun together this weekend," Alyssa said, lifting one shoulder.

"So, for real . . . do you like him?" Grace asked.

Jenna looked around at all their faces. They didn't look very happy about this conversation, and she knew why. If Jenna admitted that she liked David, it was going to cause a huge problem between her and Sarah. Which meant that there would be a huge problem in their bunks this summer. That was the last thing anyone wanted.

"Because if you do like him, you might want to tell Sarah," Valerie said. "She has the right to know."

Jenna suddenly felt as if she was being questioned by the police or something. They were all looking at her as if they already thought she was guilty. Clearly they had discussed this behind her back already—a lot. And it seemed like they had decided that Jenna was in the wrong.

"Look, you guys, I do not like David," Jenna said firmly. "We're only hanging out together because of the olde-tyme competition. If it wasn't for that stupid boy-girl pair rule, I wouldn't even be talking to him."

"Yeah. You just keep telling yourself that," Tori said, tossing her blond ponytail over her shoulder.

"What's that supposed to mean?" Jenna snapped.

Tori paled slightly. "It's just that . . . Jenna, we've seen the way you look at him, you know, when you think no one is watching?"

Jenna felt as if she was going to be sick.

"You definitely look like a girl with a crush," Natalie put in.

"Well, what do you guys know?" Jenna fumed. "You think you're so smart just because you come from New York and L.A.? Well, you don't know everything. And I'm telling you I *don't* like him. What do you want me to do? Prove it to you?"

No one said anything. Jenna knew she was getting kind of loud, but so what? She was mad. Her friends were all accusing her of going behind Sarah's back to steal her boyfriend. She would never do that. No matter how much she liked him. And even though he'd already *told* her that *he* liked *her*.

"Fine. I'll prove it to you," Jenna said.

"How?" Alyssa asked.

"Don't worry about it," Jenna told her. "I have my ways."

Just then the first firework jetted into the sky, letting out a loud whistle. It popped overhead, sending a blanket of blue and white sparkles over the sky. Everyone around Jenna's blanket oohed and aahed.

"Let's just watch the fireworks," Jenna grumbled.

Gradually all the other girls settled back, tipping their faces toward the sky. Grace turned off her flashlight and closed her book. Alex lay down next to Jenna, looking as if she would rather be curled up in bed. With a sigh, Jenna lay back as well and tried to get into the beautiful display in the sky above, but her mind kept wandering.

She had to show her friends that she did not like David once and for all. There was no way she could handle having this conversation *again*. They had to know for sure that there was no way she would ever stab Sarah—or any of them—in the back that way. It was time to come up with a plan. A really good plan . . .

chapter

TEN

That night, Jenna lay on her side in her sleeping bag, staring at the legs on the dresser near the wall. Her eyes were wide open and she listened carefully, waiting for everyone to fall asleep. After several summers sleeping every night in a bunk full of girls, she had learned to recognize the signs. Slowed breathing, loud snorts, the occasional twitch. After about twenty minutes, all her friends were officially down for the count.

Ever so carefully, Jenna slipped her legs out of her sleeping bag and pushed herself up. Tori, who was sleeping next to her, stirred and turned over, but didn't wake. Quickly, Jenna tiptoed across the room. Being the ultimate prankster, her sneaking skills were top-notch, and she was feeling quite proud of herself. Until she stepped right on Grace's textbook and slid halfway across the room. Somehow she managed not to shout in surprise, but her heart hit her throat. The book smacked into the wall, and Jenna lost her balance and fell on her bottom on the hardwood floor.

She winced and looked around quickly, holding her breath. No open eyes. No one staring at her. She was still safe.

She got up and picked up the book. Darn slick covers. Then she brought it into the bathroom with her so that it wouldn't cause any more trouble.

Luckily, Jenna had never removed the nightlight her mother had put in the bathroom when she was little. Even though it was kind of childish, it was good for finding her way to the bathroom in the middle of the night. Now she was extra glad to have it because it meant she didn't have to risk turning the light on and waking everyone.

Jenna placed Grace's book in the magazine basket next to the toilet and opened the medicine cabinet. She grabbed the box of hair dye that Alyssa had found on Friday night and held the directions up to the nightlight. Before bed, everyone had been in and out of the bathroom, brushing their teeth and combing their hair, so she hadn't had time to read the directions then. Now she scanned them quickly, just hoping they wouldn't be too complex. If the dye required the use of a hairdryer or something, her plan was toast.

"Perfect," Jenna whispered to herself, her heart fluttering with excitement.

The kit was just for streaking, so all she had to do was brush the dye on with the little applicator that was included. This was definitely going to work. She quickly opened the box and took out the bottle and brush. Then she took the box and stuffed it into the bottom of the garbage can, covering it over with tissues and cotton balls.

Biting her lip to keep from grinning, Jenna clutched the hair dye and crept through the room again. This time she was even more careful and she made it to the door without a trip. Quietly, she slipped out into the hallway and closed the door behind her. Then she raced down the carpeted hall to Adam and David's room. When she saw that their door was already open, she could barely contain her giggle.

What was wrong with these guys? At the very least, they should have expected Jenna and her friends to try to get them back for the Silly String attack. But they hadn't even bothered to close and lock their door. It was like they were asking for it.

Slowly, Jenna stepped inside. The light from the full moon outside illuminated the room just enough so that Jenna could see. Adam was all curled up on one bed with the covers in a ball at his feet. David lay peacefully sleeping on his back on the other bed.

Jenna's pulse pounded with excitement. She tiptoed over to David's side and knelt down next to his bed, her knees on the rattan throw rug. He didn't move a muscle. Just kept breathing slowly and steadily.

This is too easy, Jenna told herself giddily.

She unscrewed the top of the hair-dye bottle and squeezed a bit of the smelly liquid onto the brush. She was just about to touch the brush to David's hair when she made the mistake of looking at his face.

His totally cute, unsuspecting, sleeping face.

Guilt overcame her. She and David had been

having so much fun the past couple of days. He had been so sweet and so funny. And he had told her he liked her. No guy had ever told her that before. Could she really do this to him?

Then she thought of Sarah. Yes, David had told her that he liked her, but he had done it while he was still dating Sarah. He was a pig! A jerk and a pig and a jerk some more. She *could* do this to him. He totally deserved it. No matter how cute he looked while he was sleeping.

With a deep breath, Jenna touched the brush to David's hair and got to work.

▲ ▲ ▲

The next morning, Jenna and her friends were out on the back deck bright and early, getting ready for their final rehearsal before the talent competition. Val was leading everyone in stretching, but Jenna was always one step behind. She kept glancing over her shoulder at the sliding doors to the house, wondering when David was going to wake up.

"Jenna! We're doing our arms now," Val said impatiently.

Jenna popped her head up from her calf stretch and smiled. "Sorry. Just . . . feeling the burn!"

Everyone laughed and rolled their eyes. Jenna looked at the doors again. Her heart jumped when they slid open, then fell when she saw that it was only Grace.

"Found it!" she said, holding up her textbook. "Anyone know why it was in the bathroom?"

"Maybe you were sleepwalking with it," Brynn joked.

"Actually, I stepped on it when I went to the bathroom in the middle of the night," Jenna said. "That thing is a menace."

"Tell me about it," Grace said, blowing out a sigh. "Sorry if it got in your way."

Jenna recalled how she had almost cracked her head open the night before—and alerted everyone to her latest prank—and smiled. "Not a problem. I didn't know you were looking for it or I would have told you where it was."

"Believe me, part of me did not want to find it," Grace told her.

Suddenly the girls heard a shout from inside and Jenna's heart slammed into her ribcage. A window slid open overhead and Adam pressed his face into the screen.

"Jenna! What did you do!?" he cried.

All Jenna's friends turned to look at her. They were all very well aware of her long prankster tradition. With everyone staring at her, Jenna had a hard time keeping a straight face.

"Jenna . . ." Alex said in a scolding tone.

"What? I'm innocent," Jenna said.

Two seconds later the back door slid open and out ran David, still in his pajama pants and T-shirt. His hair was sticking straight up from his head and it was striped with blue. He looked hilarious, but the best part was the blue eyebrows. Jenna had thought of it at the last minute before leaving his room. She had been scared out of her mind that he would wake up the entire time she was working on them, but he hadn't. The results were totally worth the effort. He looked absolutely insane.

"Jenna! Omigod!" Natalie cried, putting her hand over her mouth.

Everyone cracked up laughing. Val even doubled over, she was laughing so hard. Jenna was overwhelmed by a feeling of total triumph. They thought she liked David? Ha! Would she really do *that* to a guy that she *liked?*

"You did this to me?" David blurted, walking over to Jenna.

Jenna grinned back at him. "I admit nothing."

She waited for him to freak out and yell at her. She waited for him to demand that she fix it. But instead, he backed up a few steps and smiled.

"Well I . . . *love* it!" he cried. He placed his fists on his hips and looked up at the sky, all regal. "I am The Blue Menace!" he shouted, hamming it up. "You will all bow in the face of my extreme blue power!"

"Omigosh. He's nuts," Alex said. "He's completely and totally nuts."

David walked over to the CD player and hit the play button. The second the music started he launched into a silly superhero dance, thrusting his arms over his head and pretending to fly around the deck. Jenna was stunned. David wasn't mad at all. He was, in fact, enjoying this.

So much for getting him back for telling her he liked her. If anything, she had made his day.

All the girls laughed and clapped to the beat as David continued with his silly show. Even Jenna couldn't help cracking up when he jumped up on a chair and wagged his hips back and forth. This was great. She liked a guy who had a good sense of humor—a guy who could take a joke. David was even cooler than she had thought.

The moment Jenna realized this, her heart fell. Thanks to her little prank, she had just discovered something *else* she liked about David.

This whole plan had really blown up in her face.

chapter

ELEVEN

"Why didn't I think of this before?" Valerie wailed, standing in the center of the guest room after lunch. "What are we going to wear?"

"We'll look like total losers if we don't have costumes," Tori agreed.

Jenna looked around the guest room, which looked as if a department store had exploded all over it. Everyone had pulled out all their clothes, and they were arranging them on the beds to see if anything would work.

"You guys will come up with something," Jenna said, patting Val on the back. "This is the most creative bunch of people on the planet."

Valerie looked at Jenna, her forehead all wrinkled. "I'm so sorry we won't be able to come to the water-balloon toss to cheer for you," she said. "But we have to figure this out."

"It's okay," Jenna said.

Jenna would have loved to have stayed to help, but she *was* supposed to be competing in the water-balloon toss with David in a few minutes. They still had a chance to win the olde-tyme competition if they took first or second place.

Unfortunately, Jenna wasn't even sure if she wanted to be around David right now. She had a feeling it was just going to be awkward and awful. That morning she had even entertained the idea of quitting the competition, but that had lasted all of five seconds. Quitting was not Jenna's style, especially when she had such a good shot at winning.

Still, it would have been really nice to have even *one* friend there to back her up and cheer her on.

"Are you sure *none* of you can come?" Jenna asked, looking hopefully at Brynn.

"I would, Jen, but I kind of want to be here for Alex," Brynn whispered, glancing over her shoulder at where Alex was helping Alyssa sort clothes. "She and Adam haven't said a word to each other all day, so she's not going to compete."

Jenna took a deep breath. She knew that Brynn was right. Alex really did need her more than Jenna did right now. It looked like she was just going to have to be brave and head to the competition on her own.

"Okay. Well then, I guess I'll see you guys at the show," Jenna said, the butterflies in her stomach going crazy.

"We'll bring your costume there," Natalie told her, holding up a black T-shirt to inspect it. "If we have one."

"Okay, well, good luck!" Jenna said, heading for the door.

"You too! Break a leg!" her friends called after her. Jenna closed the door behind her and looked down at her skinny legs sticking out of her shorts. Breaking a leg might not be a bad idea. Then she wouldn't have to go through with this whole thing. But, of course, she knew that wasn't *actually* an option. Nope. She was going to have to face David. With a water balloon.

Taking a deep breath, Jenna turned and started down the stairs. Time to get this over with.

▲ ▲ ▲

A huge crowd had gathered to watch the water-balloon toss. So huge that for a second Jenna was worried she might not even be able to find David. But then she saw a shock of blue hair and snorted a laugh. Like he would ever be difficult to find with *that* hairdo.

Her knees quaking, Jenna walked up behind David and poked him twice on the shoulder. He turned around and smiled. He had a blue water balloon in one hand. Very color-coordinated.

"Hey! I was starting to think maybe you weren't going to show," he said.

"Like I would miss this," Jenna said. She noticed that a bunch of people around them were pointing and staring. And laughing. Her mouth twisted into a smirk. "That's a good look for you," she told him.

"Ya think?" he said, touching his hair with his free hand. "Maybe you should try it. Problem is, I have no idea who my stylist is, so I can't tell you who to go to."

His eyes were dancing as he looked at Jenna. She felt her skin start to grow warm and shrugged.

"That's too bad."

"Jenna, come on. I know you did this to me," David said.

"Me? Please! Where would *I* get blue hair dye?" Jenna said automatically. "Have you *seen* me go to a store this weekend?"

David laughed. "I don't know how you did it, I just know you did. And I think I know why, too."

Jenna's stomach twisted into knots and she looked away.

"I think you did it because—"

"All competitors, please take your places on the white lines!" the announcer's voice boomed over the loudspeakers. "That's right, line up across from your partner on the white lines!"

"Gotta go!" Jenna said, more than happy to put an end to their conversation.

She jogged over to the white line farthest from her and turned to face David. Gradually everyone else fell into place. Jenna was glad to see that Adam hadn't shown up. If he'd come here thinking that Alex would be here and then Alex hadn't arrived, Adam would have been crushed.

The announcer stepped up to the end of the two lines of competitors. He was wearing a tremendous red cowboy hat with a blue ribbon around it. His red, white, and blue plaid cowboy shirt looked as if it was about to burst at the seams trying to hold his jolly stomach.

"Everybody got a balloon?" the announcer asked.

David and all the other balloon-tossers on his

side held up their balloons.

"Okay. You know how this works," the announcer said. "You toss the balloon to your partner. He or she catches it and throws it back. If you get through that without a splash, then the person holding the balloon takes one step back and it starts all over again. Whoever finishes this thing dry is our winner."

The crowd laughed as one and the announcer beamed.

"All righty, then. On your marks! Get set! Toss!" he shouted.

Jenna got ready to catch. All the balloons flew. All except David's. He looked at Jenna and smiled.

"What are you doing? Toss your balloon!" she said through her teeth.

"I think you did it because you like me," David said.

All the color drained out of Jenna's face.

"What? Why would I do *that* to someone I liked?" Jenna said.

"Exactly!"

David tossed the balloon underhand to Jenna. She was still so stunned by what he'd said to her that she almost dropped it. Almost.

"You're not making any sense," she said.

"I think you did it because you like me and you were trying to make me and everyone else think that you don't," David said with a triumphant smirk. "Am I right?"

Jenna's jaw dropped. He was, of course, right. But she couldn't believe he was saying all of this to her.

Right here in front of all these people! Thank goodness her friends had decided not to come. This could have been even more awful than it already was.

"I knew it! I am right!" David cheered.

Then Jenna pulled back and flung the water balloon right at his feet as hard as she possibly could. The balloon popped and splashed water all up David's legs and onto his shirt. He closed his eyes and wiped a few drops of water off his cheek.

"Uh-oh! There goes our first couple!" the announcer called out.

David stared at Jenna and grinned. "You are *so* dead!"

He turned and ran over to a huge bucket holding dozens of water balloons. Jenna's eyes widened and she started to run, but it was too late. Suddenly a balloon exploded on her back, soaking her T-shirt and shorts. A bunch of the competitors sprang away.

"I can't believe you did that!" Jenna cried.

She raced over to the bucket, cutting David off from it.

"Now, now, now!" the announcer called out. "This is not a water-balloon *fight*."

"It is now!" Jenna shouted.

She grabbed two balloons, one in each hand, and backed up. The moment she was clear of the bucket, David did the same. They circled each other, ammunition at the ready, each waiting for the other to make their move. David kept balking—pretending he was about to throw—and every time he did, Jenna flinched and shrieked. Finally she couldn't take it anymore. She pulled back and let her first balloon fly. It glanced off David's shoulder and bounced harmlessly to the grass.

"Darn it!" Jenna shouted.

"You missed me! You missed me!" David taunted.

Jenna narrowed her eyes and immediately threw her second balloon. This time she got him right in the chest and the balloon exploded. David closed his eyes as water dripped from his chin. Jenna laughed.

"Oh! Is someone all wet?" Jenna said, pretending to pout.

"Nice one," David said, opening his eyes. "But now you're unarmed."

He pulled his arm back and ran right at her. Jenna screamed and sprinted away. The crowd parted, people jumping left and right to keep out of the line of fire. Jenna finally made it to a huge oak tree near the edge of the field and crouched behind it.

"You can't stay back there forever!" David called out.

"Oh, yes I can!" Jenna shouted back, laughing.

A balloon slammed into the bark right next to her left arm, soaking her all over again. Jenna ran right and found herself face-to-face with David. He held up the second water balloon. Her heart pounded right through her T-shirt. How could he be all blue-haired and drenched and *still* be cute?

"Aren't I soaked enough?" she asked.

"I won't use it if you admit it," David said with a smile. "Admit you like me."

"No!" Jenna said, but she couldn't stop grinning.

David lifted the balloon over his head. Jenna backed into the tree. Her curls were plastered to her face and neck, and her soaked T-shirt clung uncomfortably to her arms. "Admit it!" he said.

"Never!" Jenna said.

"Admit it or it's soak city," David sang, waving the balloon around.

Jenna did not want to get hit with another balloon. She was already drenched and she had to be onstage right after this. Valerie was going to freak out as it was. If she showed up in even worse shape, the girl might faint.

"Okay, fine! Fine!" Jenna shouted, throwing her hands up. "I admit it, okay? I like you, too."

The moment she said it, Jenna felt awful. How had she gotten into this totally horrible situation? What would Sarah think if she saw what was happening right now?

David dropped his arm. "You do?"

"Yeah! I do!" Jenna snapped, angry at herself. All her blood rushed to her face. "But it doesn't matter! You're with Sarah. And I could never do that to a friend."

David's face fell. "But I told you I don't like Sarah that way anymore."

Jenna felt her shoulders slump along with her heart. "It doesn't matter. Sarah is my friend and as long as you're with her, I can't be around you. So please, just . . . leave me alone."

"You guys, this girl is really good," Alex said, coming backstage from the wings where she had been listening to the solo singer out onstage. Watching the other performers was the only thing keeping her mind off her nerves. And off of Adam. "I think she was actually on *American Idol* last year. In the preliminary rounds, I mean."

"Well that's not fair," Brynn said. "Once you get on *A.I.*, there should be some law that you can't do local competitions anymore."

"Totally," Grace agreed.

"Where on earth is Jenna?" Valerie asked, clutching her hands together. "We're going on in ten minutes!"

"Maybe she and David won," Alex suggested hopefully. "Maybe they had to pose for pictures or something."

"Not exactly."

Everyone turned around at the sound of Jenna's voice. She had just walked in through the back door and she was soaking wet from head to toe. Her hair was a matted, dripping mess, and her pink T-shirt looked like it had just been used to wash a car.

"What happened to you?" Alex asked, her heart going out to Jenna. The girl couldn't have looked more miserable if she tried.

"We lost. Big-time," Jenna said.

"Oh! I'm so sorry, Jenna!" Grace said. "We know how much you wanted to win that competition."

Grace went to hug Jenna and both Alex and Val shrieked. "Don't!" Val said. "You'll get all wet!"

"Shhhh!" one of the other waiting competitors scolded them.

Jenna and Grace stared at Val like she was nuts.

"Sorry. It's just that we spent all morning coming up with these costumes. They're the only ones we've got," Val said sheepishly.

All the girls were wearing either a black T-shirt or a white T-shirt and denim bottoms—jeans, shorts, or skirts. Alyssa had found an old black-and-white paisley sheet and had asked Mr. Bloom if she could tear it up. He had no problem with it, so Alyssa had cut the sheet into strips and made headbands with them. Alex thought their outfits looked pretty cool—not at all like they had just thrown the whole thing together. But Valerie was right. If Grace's costume got wet, there was nothing to replace it.

"Come on," Natalie said, hooking her arm around Jenna's. "Let's go get you dried off."

Tori grabbed Jenna's costume and her makeup bag and followed after them to the bathroom. Alex wanted to go with them and ask Jenna if Adam had shown up for the balloon toss. She was kind of dying to know. But she figured that now was not the best time.

A few minutes later, *American Idol*–girl was done with her song and bowing for her standing ovation. Jenna and the other girls returned from the bathroom and Jenna looked ten times better. Her hair was still wet, but it had been slicked back into a ponytail with her headband holding her curls in place. She wore a fitted black T-shirt and denim shorts, and Tori had brushed on some eye shadow and blush.

"Jenna, you look great," Val said. "There's only one more act before ours. Is everybody ready?"

"Yeah!" they all whispered.

Greg, the show's director, stepped up to them with his clipboard. "Valerie! You girls should be in the wings," he whispered. "You're up next."

Alex's skin sizzled with nerves.

"Okay, girls! Let's do this!" Val said.

Alex was about to follow the others over to the wings when a bright shaft of light hit her and she turned around. Her heart dropped straight to her toes. Adam had just walked in through the back door.

"Alex!" he whispered. "Can I talk to you?"

"No," Alex said, her heart pounding. "We're about to go on."

"Do you have just a second?" Adam asked. "It's really important. You never gave me a chance to say anything yesterday and I want to explain."

Alex felt as if she was going to have a seriously premature heart attack. Between her fear of going out onstage and this, she was sure she was going to keel over.

"Fine," she whispered. "But it has to be fast."

Adam took her arm and gently tugged her toward the wall. "Listen, I'm really sorry if you got the idea that I only like you some of the time," he said, his brown eyes sincere. "It's just . . . it's . . ."

"What?" Alex prompted.

"It's my dad," Adam admitted, looking miserable.

Alex blinked. That was the last thing she had ever thought he would say. "Your dad?" Did Adam and

Jenna's father not like her or something?

"Yeah. He's everywhere," Adam said, lifting a shoulder. "And, I don't know, but I feel really weird whenever he's around. You know, my girlfriend and my dad in the same place . . . I don't know how to act around you when he's there. It's just . . . a little too close for comfort."

Alex thought back to the times that Adam had ignored her that weekend. First it was out on the porch when he'd arrived and his dad had come up behind him. Then it was when they were setting the table and his dad was there. Then it was at the gazebo when his father had been standing right next to him. And all the times he'd been nice to her, his father wasn't anywhere nearby.

Suddenly everything made sense. And Alex felt totally silly for jumping to conclusions.

"So that's why I was acting weird," Adam told her. "I just wanted you to know."

He bowed his head and turned to go.

"Adam! Wait," Alex said.

He turned around, a hopeful look on his face.

"I'm so sorry," Alex said. "I totally understand."

"You do?" Adam said with a smile.

"Are you kidding?" Alex said. "I never thought about it before, but I have no idea what I would do if I had to be around you and my parents at the same time."

The very thought made her shudder.

"I'm sorry I didn't think of it," Alex said.

"I'm sorry I didn't tell you sooner," Adam replied.

"So . . . will you be my girlfriend again?"

Alex's heart fluttered with happiness and she grinned. "Definitely."

"Cool. 'Cause soon we'll be at camp and then I won't have to worry about my dad," Adam said. "Except, you know, on Parents' Day."

They both laughed.

"Alex! We're on!" Valerie whispered, sticking her head around the corner.

"I gotta go!" Alex said.

"Hang on," Adam said. Then he leaned forward and kissed her on the cheek. Alex felt a warm rush go straight through her entire body. "Break a leg," Adam told her.

"Thanks," Alex said.

Then she turned and practically skipped over into the wings, joining the rest of her friends.

"You look happy," Natalie said.

"We made up!" Alex announced happily. "Me and Adam. We're back together."

"Yay!" Brynn cheered, throwing her arms around Alex.

"That's so great, Alex," Alyssa said.

"I'm really happy for you, Alex," Jenna told her, giving her a squeeze.

"Thanks. Know what I feel like doing right now?" Alex said.

"What?" Tori asked.

"Getting out there and kicking a little dance butt," Alex said.

The girls laughed.

"I don't know if that's technically possible," Val said.

Alex shrugged. "Let's do it anyway."

The girls all cheered and hugged and then Greg stepped out onstage and announced their act.

"And now, give it up for the Camp Lakeview Dancers!" he cried.

With one last encouraging grin for her friends, Alex bounded out onto the stage.

TWELVE

Valerie grinned as she spun around and jutted out her hip, throwing herself right into the last dance sequence. Nova's song sounded even more incredible on the huge sound system and the crowd was on its feet, clapping to the beat. Their enthusiasm psyched Valerie up even more, and she knew she was dancing her best and so was everyone else. The audience was totally loving it.

The five judges sat at their table near the front of the crowd and they definitely looked impressed. Valerie made sure to make eye contact with them and smile as much as possible. She saw one of the women make a note on her clipboard and wondered what she was writing. Then Valerie realized she didn't care. She was having so much fun, it didn't matter what the judges thought. All that mattered was that she had done her best.

Together as one, the eight friends threw their arms up, striking their last pose. The roar of the crowd was overwhelming.

"We did it!" Natalie cheered, running over to Val for a hug.

Val bear-hugged her back. "We so did!"

As everyone else crowded around her, hugging and jumping up and down and squealing, Valerie couldn't believe it. They had actually pulled it off. Even with all the insanity, they had put on a great show. She looked at Jenna, who was grinning like mad, and Alex, who was whooping and hollering. Even Grace was laughing and rosy-cheeked. Somehow they had all put their personal stuff aside and come together. Win or lose, Valerie couldn't have been more proud. Or grateful. Her friends had known how important the talent competition was to her and they had really come through.

"Let's hear it for the Camp Lakeview Dancers!" Greg announced.

The crowd cheered again, but no one cheered louder than Valerie and her friends as they jogged offstage together. It was a perfect moment—one Val knew she was going to remember forever.

A little while later, Valerie found herself onstage again, holding hands on her left with Alex and on her right with Jenna. All the contestants were lined up under the stage lights, which seemed almost unnecessary with the sun shining the way it was. The judges were clumped together, whispering to one another, making their final decisions.

Valerie couldn't believe that this was it. After all that preparation, it was already over and soon they would know who had won. Then, in just over an hour, her friends would all be saying good-bye to one another again. The weekend had just blown by. Thinking about it almost made Valerie's spirits start to droop, but then she remembered where she was and what she was doing.

And her stomach twisted into nervous knots all over again.

"Do you think we have a shot?" Jenna whispered.

"Definitely," Valerie said with confidence. "As good a shot as anyone else."

"I don't know. That *American Idol* girl . . ." Alex said.

"She was good, but she wasn't all that," Valerie replied.

She quickly looked up and down the line of performers. Aside from the solo singer, there were ten other acts. There was a pair of tap-dancing boys a couple of years younger than Val and her friends who had been really good and had won the crowd over with their sheer cuteness. There was a juggler and a flutist and a magician and a guitarist—plus that guy who had jumped up and down on a pogo stick while reciting Shakespeare. That had just been weird.

A few of the acts had been good, but Valerie thought the crowd had cheered louder for her and her friends than for anyone else. There was definitely a good chance they could at least place.

"Here we go!" Tori whispered.

Valerie's nerves sizzled as the judges handed a slip of paper to Greg. He climbed up onstage and a buzz of excitement went through the line of contestants. The audience hushed and those who had been milling around took their seats. They shaded their eyes with their hands and pointed at various people onstage, guessing at who might have won.

Please let it be us! Please let it be us! Valerie thought.

"Thank you everyone for coming to this year's Memorial Day Talent Competition!" Greg said into the microphone.

The crowd and all the contestants applauded. Valerie didn't realize until that moment how much her palms were sweating. She was embarrassed to hold her friends' hands again, but they grabbed her without hesitation.

"We had a great show this year, didn't we?" Greg asked.

More applause. Valerie grinned.

"It was a rough decision for our judges, but they've managed to come up with a third-place, second-place, and first-place winner," Greg said. "And I know our contestants are dying to hear the results—"

Everyone laughed nervously.

"So without further ado, let's start with third place," Greg said, glancing behind him at the contestants. "Our third-place winners are . . ."

Winners. That means it's a group, Valerie thought. *Maybe we won third place!*

Val wasn't sure whether to be psyched or disappointed at the idea of third.

"Robbie and Ronnie Jackson!" Greg announced.

The two tap dancers cheered and raced up to

grab their yellow ribbons, their tap shoes clip-clopping on the stage. The audience roared for them and all the contestants clapped. Then Val found her hands clasped in Jenna's and Alex's again.

Her heart pounded in her ears. She could feel all her friends trying not to jump out of their skin. Jenna's leg bounced up and down like mad.

"Our second-place winner is . . . Bernadette Childress!" Greg announced.

"Yes!" Alex cheered.

Bernadette, the solo singer, looked stunned. Valerie got the feeling that she thought she was going to win first place. So had Valerie, actually. Finally Bernadette came forward and took her red ribbon with a smile.

"We really have a chance now," Natalie whispered.

"Shh! You'll jinx it!" Grace cried.

Valerie couldn't have talked to save her life. She was too nervous and excited.

"And finally, our first-place winners, who win not only blue ribbons, but get to take home this lovely trophy," Greg said, picking up the gold and faux-marble trophy from the table at the corner of the stage. "This year's talent champions . . . the Camp Lakeview Dancers!"

Valerie and all her friends screamed at the top of their lungs. The entire audience laughed. Val hugged Jenna and Alex, then everyone else in turn, before running up to claim the trophy.

"We won! We won!" Brynn shouted over and over again.

"Valerie! You are the best choreographer *ever!*" Alyssa cheered. "You did it!"

"We *all* did it!" Valerie cheered.

"Yeah we did!" Jenna shouted, thrusting her blue ribbon in the air.

"Hey! This time we *both* won something!" Alex cried, high-fiving Jenna.

"Winning is always better together," Jenna agreed.

Valerie beamed. It was the perfect ending to a perfect weekend. Alex and Jenna got to go home champions of something after all, Grace knew her history backward and forward, and Valerie had gotten to do her favorite thing—dance. Plus everyone else seemed pretty darn happy, too.

Alyssa handed Greg her camera and asked him to take a picture of the group. Everyone gathered around the trophy as Greg held the camera up.

"Say winners!" he instructed.

"Winners!" Valerie and her friends cried.

▲ ▲ ▲

Jenna sat with her seven friends out on the porch in front of the house, their bags placed all around them. Any minute now the parents and Tori's driver would be arriving to take everyone back home. Jenna couldn't believe how quickly the weekend had gone by. She had looked forward to it for so long and now it was already over. She also couldn't believe everything that had happened in just a few days. Alex and Adam had broken up and gotten back together. Grace was now an expert in Civil War history. They had all choreographed, perfected, and performed a whole dance routine. And they had won first prize in the talent competition.

Not to mention that little mutual confession of *like* between herself and David. Jenna squirmed in her seat just thinking about it.

"Jenna, is something wrong?" Alyssa asked. "You've been quiet all afternoon."

"Yeah, and we won first place," Brynn said. "Wouldn't you usually be nonstop cheering about that?"

Jenna looked at her friends and sighed. Maybe telling them would help. It wasn't like she could keep it a secret. These things always had a way of getting out. After all her summers at camp, she knew that better than anyone.

"David told me he liked me," she confessed.

"What!?" at least five people screeched at one time.

"Shhhhhh!" Jenna said, looking over her shoulder. David and Adam were all the way down at the lake, but sound carried around here. "It gets worse," she said, gulping. "I told him I liked him back."

Brynn and Grace lost all the color in their cheeks. Alex looked positively green. Val blew out a sigh and shook her head. Alyssa, Natalie, and Tori exchanged concerned glances.

They all hate me. I knew it, Jenna thought.

"You guys were right all along, okay? I admit it. But we're not gonna do anything about it," Jenna assured them. "I told him that Sarah is my friend and I can't, like, go out with her boyfriend behind her back or something."

"What did he say?" Alyssa asked.

"Nothing," Jenna said miserably. "I kind of told him to stay away from me, then ran away." She hugged her legs up to her chest and hid her face behind her knees, unable to look at them staring at her anymore. "You all think I'm a jerk now, don't you?"

"No!" they all chorused.

Natalie got up and then sat down next to Jenna, squeezing the two of them in between the arms of her chair. "Jen, we do not think you're a jerk," she said. "You can't help how you feel."

"I know! I really can't!" Jenna cried.

"It's David who's acting not-so-nice," Tori pointed out. "If he was going to tell you he liked you, he should have at least broken up with Sarah first. That would be the honorable thing to do."

"Honorable?" Alyssa asked.

"I read a lot of romance fiction," Tori said, raising one shoulder.

Alyssa smiled. "She's right, Jenna. If anything, you did the *right* thing. You told the truth, but you were also loyal to your friend."

"Just like you *always* are," Grace said.

Jenna slowly started to smile. The hard rock that had been sitting in the pit of her stomach all day finally started to melt. "Thanks, guys," she said.

Just then a station wagon pulled up the rocky drive and its horn honked. Mr. Bloom walked out the front door and let the screen door slam behind him.

"Looks like your chariots are arriving, ladies," Mr. Bloom said.

"Yep! That's my mom!" Alyssa said, jumping up.

"And *my* ride!" Grace added. She stood up and lifted her heavy text. "I can't believe we're already going home!"

"I know. I hate saying good-bye," Brynn said.

"But it's not good-bye for long," Alex pointed out. "We're all going to be at camp again in just a few weeks!"

"Yeah!" Natalie and Jenna cheered, then laughed.

"If I pass my test," Grace said, biting her lip.

"You are *so* going to pass," Valerie told her. "Just keep singing!"

Grace laughed and hugged everyone good-bye, then Alyssa did the same. Mr. Bloom, who had walked over to Alyssa's mother's car, backed up to let the girls by. They thanked him for the weekend, then piled into the car. Jenna and the rest of the girls waved at the station wagon until it was completely out of sight. As soon as the dust had settled, a black sedan pulled in, followed by Natalie's mother's SUV. Nat's mother was taking Alex, Brynn, and Val all back to New York City, where their parents would be picking them up.

"Guess everyone's going," Jenna said sadly.

"Turn that frown upside down!" Brynn told her. "You just hosted the best Lakeview reunion *ever*!"

Jenna grinned. "I did kind of do that, didn't I?"

She hugged Brynn just as Adam and David came running up from the lake. The moment Jenna saw

David, her heart started to slam around in her chest. He looked at her, blushed, and quickly looked away. Then Adam went over to Alex and they walked off together to say good-bye. That just made the vibe in the air even *more* awkward.

"Good luck on the ride home," Tori whispered to Jenna as she hugged her. "E-mail me as soon as you get there and tell me how it went. I won't get it until I land, but I'm definitely going to want to hear all about it."

"I will. I promise," Jenna told her.

Tori waved to everyone and headed for her car. Her driver got out and opened the door for her and she slipped into the backseat.

"That's the life," Brynn said. "When I'm a huge movie star, I'm totally going to roll like that."

Jenna and the rest of the girls laughed. They all hugged good-bye and soon enough, Jenna was standing there alone. With Adam and David.

"So? Everyone ready to go?" Jenna's dad asked, clapping his hands together.

"Definitely!" Jenna cried.

She ran past David, grabbed her duffel bag, and raced for the car. It took her all of two seconds to toss her stuff in the trunk, pop her headphones in her ears, and hunker down in the front seat.

When David and Adam walked over to get in the back, she avoided their gaze and turned up the volume on her MP3 player. Tori wanted to know how the ride went? As far as Jenna was concerned, all she'd have to tell Tori was that she listened to music and didn't even realize David was there.

Now if only she could get her heart to stop pounding and her palms to stop sweating. Then everything would be just *perfect*.

chapter THIRTEEN

Jenna's dad had barely hit the brakes in front of her mom's house and she was already out the door.

"Bye, Dad! Thanks! I'll call you later!" she shouted, running up the steps.

David's mom wasn't coming to pick him up for another hour, but she figured if she could just get to her room and close the door, she'd be safe.

"Hey! Jenna!" David called after her. "Wait up!"

Jenna's heart hit her throat. Her hand was already on the doorknob. She pushed the door open.

"Jenna! Come on! Stop!" David said.

"Jenna Bloom! What has gotten into you?" her dad shouted after her.

Finally Jenna stopped in her tracks. She turned around and faced David, who was right behind her on the front stairs. Her father and Adam were still back at the car, unloading bags and looking at Jenna and David like they were crazy.

Maybe they're right, Jenna thought, trying to catch her breath.

"You didn't say one thing to me on the whole car ride," David said. "What's up?"

"What's up? Are you kidding me?" Jenna asked.

"So . . . what? You're never going to talk to me again?" David asked, looking sad and hopeful at the same time.

Jenna felt all heavy inside. She wanted to talk to David. She wanted to make him laugh and hang out and maybe even dance with him again one day. Doing all of that with David was so much fun. But she couldn't. Not as long as he was going out with her friend.

"I'm sure we'll talk again at some point," she said flatly.

"You know that's not what I mean," he said, looking at her expectantly. But she wouldn't budge. "I thought you liked me."

Jenna's heart twisted painfully. Why did he have to keep bringing that up? She backed through the door and looked David in the eye. "Maybe I'll see you at camp," she said.

Then she closed the door right in his face and ran to her room as fast as she possibly could.

▲ ▲ ▲

Two nights later Jenna stared at her computer screen, feeling numb. There was an e-mail message in her inbox from Sarah, sent the morning before. Jenna could not bring herself to open it.

Clearly Sarah would be mad. Clearly she had

heard something. But what? What did she know? And how had she heard? Part of Jenna was dying to find out, but a bigger part of her was petrified to read the e-mail. If only the subject line could tip her off. But no such luck. Sarah had left it empty.

The phone rang. Jenna closed her eyes. David had already called the night before and the one before that. Both times she had told her mother to tell him she wasn't feeling well. She just hoped this wasn't him calling again.

"Jenna! It's David calling for you again!" her mother shouted up the stairs.

Jenna groaned. She got up and walked out to the hallway. "Mom? Can you just tell him I went to bed or something?"

Her mother walked over to the bottom of the stairs and looked up at Jenna, concerned. Her hand was over the telephone's mouthpiece.

"Honey? Is everything okay?" she whispered.

"Yes! I just don't want to talk to him right now. I'll . . . I'll call him back tomorrow or something," she fibbed.

"Okay," her mother said. Then she walked into the kitchen to tell the little white lie to David.

Standing in the hallway, Jenna felt totally trapped. She couldn't go back to her room and keep staring at her e-mail inbox. It was driving her crazy. She had to find out what was going on, but how was she going to do that without talking to David and without reading Sarah's e-mail?

A loud guitar wail sounded from Adam's room.

Well, there was *one* way. Jenna went over and pounded on her twin brother's door. He whipped it open. His curly hair was sticking out in all directions.

"What's up?"

"Have you talked to David since he left?" Jenna asked.

Adam broke into a wide grin. "David and Jenna sitting in a tree! K-I-S—"

Jenna slapped her hand over Adam's mouth and his eyes widened.

"Do not finish singing that song if you want to live," she said.

Adam nodded mutely. She let him go. All she could feel was the nervous pounding of her heart.

"I can't believe you like David and David likes you," Adam whispered. "If you guys go out it'll be like my sister is dating my best friend. Freaky."

"Yeah. Join the club," Jenna said.

Adam looked at her blankly.

"You and Alex?" she said.

Adam smiled and blushed. "Oh yeah. Right."

"Listen, do you know if David said anything to Sarah about him and me?" Jenna asked. "Because I have this e-mail from her and—"

"Yeah. He totally told her everything," Adam said casually. Like it was no big deal.

"He did?" Jenna said. "What did she say?"

"I'm sure she flipped out," Adam told her. "She *is* a girl."

Jenna staggered back a couple of steps until her back hit the wall.

"She flipped? He told you that?" she asked. She felt like she had just been punched in the gut.

Adam shrugged. "He didn't have to. Wouldn't *you* flip out if your friend was macking on your boyfriend?"

"Hey! I have never macked on anyone in my life!" Jenna blurted. "What does that even mean?"

"How should I know? You're the one doing it," Adam said.

"I am not!" Jenna said.

Her heart was pounding so hard she felt like it was going to explode through her chest. Adam was not telling her anything, and yet everything he said was causing her more stress.

"Anyway, why are you asking me? I thought you already know what happened," Adam said.

"Why?" Jenna asked. "Why would you think that?"

Adam rolled his eyes. "Because David *told* me Sarah was going to e-mail you," he said.

"Well, what was she going to say in the e-mail?" Jenna asked, her patience wearing thin.

Adam's brows came together. "Wait a minute. You haven't *read* that yet?"

"No," she answered.

"Well, what are you waiting for?" he asked.

"I'm . . . I'm scared, all right?" Jenna admitted. "What if she hates me?"

Adam took a deep breath. "There's only one way to find out," he said. "You gotta just open the thing, Jenna. Otherwise you're just gonna drive yourself crazy."

Jenna stared at him. If there was one thing she couldn't stand, it was when Adam made perfect sense. She tipped her head back and sighed.

"Fine! I'll open my e-mail!" she said. Then she looked at him and narrowed her eyes.

"Anytime," he told her. Then he closed the door in her face and the music started up again.

Jenna turned slowly and trudged back to her room. She dropped down in her chair and looked at the screen. Her hand was shaking as she reached for her mouse. Her throat and mouth were completely dry.

Just don't let her hate me, she thought. *Please, just don't let her hate me.*

She closed her eyes and clicked on the little, waiting envelope. After counting to ten Mississippi, she opened her eyes again and read.

To: Aries8
From: SarahSports
Subject:

Dear Jenna,

I talked to David a little while ago and he told me he didn't think we should be boyfriend and girlfriend anymore. When I asked him why, he said I wasn't going to like the reason. Then he told me he liked you now. He also told me that he told you how he feels and you shot him down. (Those were his words.) He said you told him you couldn't do that to a friend. So I just wanted to say thanks for that.

But the truth is that if you want to go out with him,

it's totally okay with me. I was going to post this on the blog, but I guess I'll tell you now: I'm not coming back to Camp Lakeview this year. Abby and I both decided to go to this sports camp that our softball coach told us about. So it won't be awkward for the three of us at camp or anything. I was probably going to break up with David anyway, since we weren't going to get to see each other this summer. So you and David can do whatever you want.

Jenna stopped reading for a moment. Her eyes had completely filled with tears, making everything blurry. She couldn't believe what she had just read. Sarah wasn't coming back to camp? That was so wrong. It was going to feel completely bizarre without her there. No Sarah on the kickball field? No Sarah and her Red Sox baseball caps? How could she just stop coming to camp? Jenna couldn't imagine it.

She took a deep breath and wiped her eyes. There were only a few lines left of the e-mail.

You've always been a really good friend, Jenna, and I'm going to miss you and Camp Lakeview SO much. I'm going to miss all our bunkmates, actually. But my softball game really needs improvement, so I think this is the right move for me.

Make sure you say hi to Dr. Steve for me! And see if you can smuggle me out some bug juice. ;-)

Love,
Sarah

Jenna took a deep breath and read the e-mail again. She just couldn't believe what she was reading. On one hand, she was relieved that Sarah didn't seem to be mad about her and David. Jenna hadn't hurt her friend after all. But on the other hand, Jenna was crushed that she wouldn't be seeing Sarah this summer. Camp Lakeview without Sarah Peyton would be like peanut butter and fluff without the fluff.

Jenna had no idea what to do next. She wanted to talk to David. She wanted to talk to Sarah. But the idea of calling either one of them made her stomach fill with butterflies. If she called David, he might ask her out, which would be totally nerve-racking. If she called Sarah, she might want to talk about the breakup, which would also be nerve-racking. Still, the urge was overwhelming. She just couldn't imagine that she might never see her friend again. That was more important than any boy. Even David.

Jenna jumped out of her chair, fished out her address book from her backpack, and ran downstairs. She grabbed the phone from the kitchen and took it into the living room. She held her breath as she dialed. Sarah picked up on the first ring.

"Hello?"

"Sarah? It's Jenna," Jenna said.

There was a pause. Jenna's heart dropped. Maybe Sarah was only pretending not to be mad at her and didn't want to talk to her ever again. Maybe that whole e-mail had been one big lie.

"Hey, Jenna! I can't believe you called!" Sarah said, sounding psyched.

Jenna's heart flooded with relief all over again. "How could I not after you told me you're not going to camp?" Jenna said. "And what's this about your softball game needing improvement? You're already the best player I know."

"Tell that to my coach. I struck out three times in the game yesterday," Sarah said.

"Ouch."

"But then I hit a two-run triple and we won," Sarah told her giddily.

"Yeah, girl!" Jenna said.

She sat back on the couch and she and Sarah chatted for twenty minutes about camp and sports and their friends. Just like old times. Jenna told Sarah all about the weekend—about what had happened between Alex and Adam and how Val had led them to victory. Sarah gave Jenna a play-by-play of her game. And neither of them ever said a word about David.

Some things were just not as important as friendship.

Posted by: Grace
Subject: I failed my test . . .

Gotcha! Just kidding! I actually got a B+! Can you believe it? I have all my bunk 4A and 4C girls to thank for that one. Of course, I did get scolded a couple of times for singing during the test . . .

But it worked! I passed history and now all I have to do is pass English and there's nothing standing between me and Camp Lakeview!

Just a few more weeks, girls! Can't wait to see you all again!

(And maybe we'll put on a little dance recital, huh?)

Turn the page for a chilling
sneak preview . . .

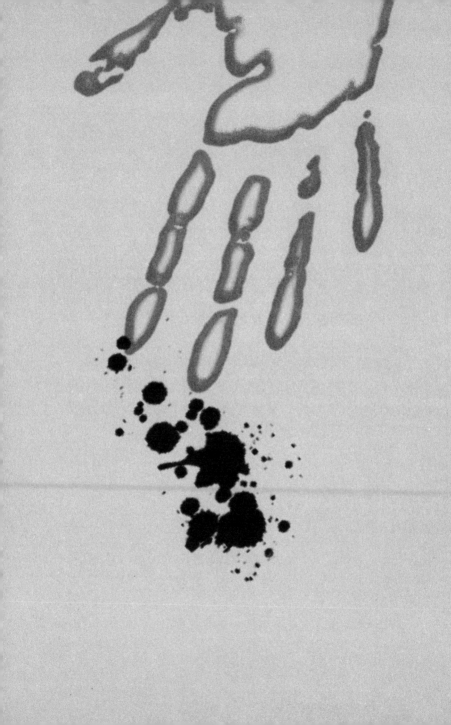

camp CONFIDENTIAL

Hide and Shriek

Available Soon!

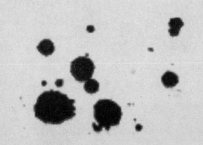

PROLOGUE

They're coming, he thought as he watched the fog slowly take form above the jagged coves and uncharted crannies of mysterious Shadow Lake.

This year, he would be ready.

I made a mistake last time. I let them get away.

The fog boiled up from the water and rolled toward him. An owl hooted beneath the bone-white moon, warning the little creatures in the dark woods that danger lurked everywhere, and they had better stay alert if they wanted to survive the night. Nature could be cruel. So could fate.

His right hand—his only hand—gripped the rotted wood of the post on the porch of the old cabin. The wood pulped between his fingers in an ooze of dry rot and decay. He was still panting from his explosion of fury.

He had been down in the basement, searching for his old ax and a couple of heads. There was so much junk down there—maps of the woods, some kid's backpack, a pair of rusted handcuffs—that he couldn't find the heads at first. Turned out they'd rolled behind the rotted couch upstairs.

He grabbed them and the ax and hurried outside. The cabin bulged with ghosts, and he couldn't stand being inside it longer than he had to. It should have been torn down long ago.

Soon, he promised himself.

His smile cracked the purple scars across his features. He turned his head slightly to the left. It was a habit he'd developed after he lost his left eye. His black eyepatch looked like an empty eye socket in the ebony darkness.

He took the first step down, then the next, and limped off the porch. The ax blade gleamed in the bone-white moonlight. He carried the heads by their hair.

When his boot touched the gritty earth, the frogs and crickets stopped singing. The owl cut short her beckoning hoot. The woods fell completely silent, and the pine boughs trembled.

The fog raced fearlessly toward him.

He limped toward shrouded Shadow Lake. His bones ached. He had been through so much. He had to get it right this time, so he could finally rest.

He had tied his old dinghy to a desiccated tree trunk that lay half submerged in the water. It looked like a bloated dead giant. The heavy fog gave it the illusion of floating in midair; it bobbed and tugged against the moor line as if it wanted to escape.

He knew the feeling.

He deposited the ax and the heads in the bow of the boat. They rolled together, then rolled apart, their eyes staring at him blankly. They were old friends. Friends he needed now, hopefully for the last time. He winked at them with his right eye. They did not wink back.

Then he held onto the tree trunk and stepped cautiously onto the slightly curved bottom of the dinghy. The craft wobbled as he found his balance. When he had first lost his arm, simple things like this had been nearly impossible to accomplish. But he had surmounted many hardships to achieve his ends. He had an iron will . . . and he didn't take failure lightly.

He clenched his jaw and slowly sat down on the seat of the boat. Then he cast off, drifting into the fog. From the bottom of the boat, he grabbed his paddle. A set of oars were useless for a man with one arm.

The flat wooden paddle cut through the water like a knife as he glided through the phantom layers of mist to the secret spot. He had hidden it well.

His single eye ticked downward through the fog to the lake, the final resting place of his hopes and dreams. If only *they* knew what lay beneath the surface of Shadow Lake. They'd be surprised. But all that belonged to the lake now.

Behind him, safely distant, the owl hooted long and low. *He's gone. It's safe to come out,* they seemed to be saying. The forest creatures skittered and darted. The woods heaved a sigh of relief.

He lifted his chin in the direction of the highway that sliced through the landscape beyond the hills and trees. It was the road they would take.

"This time, I'll get you."

And he knew that once he'd finally achieved his ends, he would disappear from Shadow Lake forever.

chapter
ONE

Dear Grace,
    Nat here! I am writing you
from the bus, which is why my handwriting is so squiggly. I've tried to
text you a gazillion times on my cell
phone, but the reception up here is not
happening. I guess it's so remote here
in rural Pennsylvania that they don't
have a lot of can-you-hear-me-now
guys making sure our phones work.
    Alyssa's on the bus. Tori, too.
She flew in last night so we could
hang in New York together. Lyss, as

usual, is writing and sketching in one of her notebooks. Tori bounced a couple rows back to talk to some kids about crops. I have no clue why she thinks that's interesting, but I'm sure she'll fill me in later. Our hot, stinky Tri-City charter has been chugging along forever, but we're almost at Camp Lake-puke. Guess how I know! We've hit that super-extra-bumpy part of the road. See? You can tell by my even worse handwriting. Plus, we just zoomed past the sign that says "Camp Lakeview 10 Miles." Witness my mad detective skills! LOL.

I wish I had brought my iPod to drown out the noise. Everyone except Lyss, Tori, and me is singing "Ninety-Nine Bottles of Beer on the Wall" for the fifth or sixth time. It's more like yelling. Even Paula Abdul would admit that the tune got lost about a hundred and thirty bottles ago.

I can't believe it's my third summer at this crazy-fun place. Do you remember our first summer together, when my mom forced me to "broaden my horizons" and shipped me out here while she went off on an art-buying trip to Europe? Remember how I freaked out? No air-conditioning, ginormous spiders and vampire mosquitoes, and <u>camp food</u>? I was ready to go back to Manhattan that very first day!

But you were so funny and friendly that I actually forgot to be miserable. Now you are one of my best Camp Lakeview Friends (CLF's for life!), and I had to actually talk my mom into <u>letting</u> me come this year instead of going with her to Asia on her art-buying trip.

Seriously, Grace, I can't wait to see you. I'm so glad you only have to miss the first two weeks of camp. You'll breeze through summer school, wait and see! English will not defeat you! After all, you passed history!

Tori's in da house! She just came back to sit with us. Now I will hear about the crops.

Oh! She wasn't listening to a conversation about <u>crops</u>, she was listening to a story about someone called <u>Cropsy</u>. She says this is the sixth year of some hideous tragedy that takes place every six years at Shadow Lake! She's going to tell Alyssa and me all about it in gory detail. Mwahaha! If it's any good, I'll give you the full 411!

See you in two weeks!

TTFN,

Nat

"Okay, I have confirmation on the dark secret of Shadow Lake."

Tori plopped down into the empty seat behind Alyssa and Natalie and leaned over their sweaty shoulders. "The story I heard is the story *they* heard. And it's all true. So, are you ready to be scared out of your wits?"

"But of course! Bring it on," Natalie said, blowing tendrils of wavy brown hair off her forehead. Despite the open windows—or perhaps because of them—it was hot and muggy inside the bus. Tori's original seatmate had gone to cram herself in with her buds at the front of the bus, so Tori had her seat all to herself. Alyssa, her dark hair pulled back in a messy bun, was sitting in front of Tori with Natalie, and they turned around to face her so they could chat.

Tori launched into her so-very-terrifying story. "Okay, so this homicidal maniac—"

"A what?" Alyssa asked, cupping her ear. "I can't hear you."

"It's about a homicidal maniac," Tori repeated, raising her voice.

Trading excited looks, Natalie and Alyssa leaned even farther over the seat to listen, and Tori noticed how much they'd changed in the last year. All three of them were definitely growing up. As ever, she and Natalie were way ahead on the trend curve in the hair and makeup departments. Tori had stylish blond Paris Hilton hair and a black T-shirt with CHIC written on it. Natalie was up-to-the-minute in her polka-dot bubble top, and they both had on fancy flip-flops decorated with bows and charms direct from Nordy's.

Alyssa appeared content to stay with her artist look of a torn T-shirt and paint-splattered jeans (in this weather!), her dark eyelashes accentuated by lots of heavy black mascara and dramatic ebony butterfly earrings. But Natalie and Alyssa's faces were a little longer and thinner, Tori noticed. More mature. It was both cool and scary at the same time.

Like my story.

"I originally heard this from my Pennsylvania cousin, Nicole," she began. Then she frowned when she saw that they were still straining to hear her. She figured it was best to unravel her creepy tale of death in a hushed, spooky tone, but two-thirds of the bus was still determined to count beer bottles backward, in song.

"I really should wait to tell it," she ventured, but both Natalie and Alyssa made sad-puppy faces.

"You can *not* stop now," Natalie insisted. "We will die of curiosity."

"You will not," Tori said, laughing. "I haven't even started!"

"Okay, maybe we won't die, but we will get very sick," Natalie insisted. "Please, please, please?"

Alyssa, the more subdued one, raised her eyebrows in a silent request.

"All right," Tori relented. "My cousin Nicole—she's way older than us—used to come here. Every summer. Then six years ago, something terrible happened . . . and she never came back again."